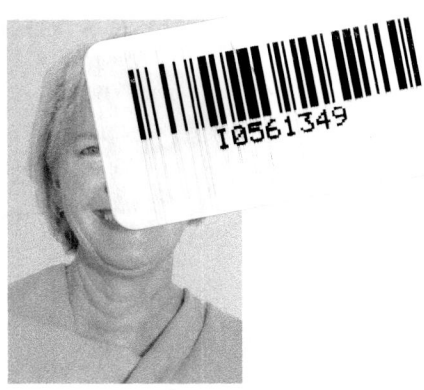

Karen grew up in a small country town in north-eastern Victoria, Australia. She spent her childhood riding horses through beautiful scenery of eucalypts, lakes, and snow-capped mountains and her love of landscape deeply affects her writing. She worked in a range of educational settings and holds a Ph.D. and M.Ed. (Hons) in the areas of fantasy. She is particularly interested in the power of the hero's inner journey which she explores through Deep Fantasy. Karen has travelled extensively overseas but enjoys nothing more than camping in the Australian Outback. She lives in Melbourne and now writes full-time. You can find out more about Karen and her books on her website.

Connect with K. S. Nikakis

Amazon: https://www.amazon.com/author/ksnikakis
Twitter: https://twitter.com/KSNikakis
Facebook: www.facebook.com/ksnikakis
Goodreads: www.goodreads.com
Website: www.ksnikakis.com
Email: author@ksnikakis.com

WORKS BY K S NIKAKIS

Non Fiction

Journey: Seeking the Sacred, Spirit and Soul in the
Australian Wilderness

Fantasy Novels
Series

Angel Caste series:
Angel Blood
Angel Breath
Angel Bone
Angel Bound
Angel Blessed
Angel Caste – Complete 5 Book Series

The Kira Chronicles trilogy:*
The Whisper of Leaves
The Song of the Silvercades
The Cry of the Marwing
remnant hard copies only

The Kira Chronicles series:
The Whisper of Leaves
The Silence of Stone
The Secrets of Stars
The Thunder of Hoofs
The Crying of Birds
The Music of Home
The Kira Chronicles – Complete 6 Book Series

Fantasy Novels

The Emerald Serpent
Heart Hunter
The Third Moon
Messenger
I Heard the Wolf Call My Name
Finalist Best YA Novel Aurealis Awards, 2019

Fantasy Short Stories

The Gift
The Tale of Prince Anura
Dragon Sprite
Glass-Heart
Finalist Best YA Short Story Aurealis Awards, 2019

Angel Caste
Book 3 Angel Bone

K.S.Nikakis

Angel Caste – Book 3 Angel Bone

First published by SOV Media Australia 2017
Amazon: www.amazon.com.au

Publisher: SOV Media
Melbourne, Australia.

Cover by AS Nikakis: http://asnikakis.com
Shutterstock.com/schankz
DaFont.com/Abdullah Alkhafaji – Ghost Theory 2

National Library of Australia
Cataloguing-in-Publication entry:
Nikakis, Karen Simpson
The Angel Caste series – Book 3 Angel Bone
ISBN 978-0-6489797-6-0

Learn more about KS Nikakis and her deep
fantasy books at: http://www.ksnikakis.com

For the Terang Gang – Lyn and Steve Keating

Glossary of the Rynth

ANGEL CASTE

Crystal Fold
Principae (*prin-sip-ay*)
Nearest to transcendence. Manifest mainly as aqua light, with white wings and group consciousness. The Principae transcend Crystal Fold to the Great Beyond.

Ezam Fold
Archae (*ar-kay*)
Five levels: angels ascend from Quin-archae through Quar-archae, Tri-archae, Du-archae, Prime-archae up to Archae. The Archae transcend Ezam Fold to Crystal Fold to become Principae, then transcend to the Great Beyond.

Members of the Archae
Archae Kald
Archae Dejon (*day-jon*)

Members of Prime-archae
Prime-archae Mirek
Prime- archae Serith

Dane
Lowest in the hierarchy and newest angels to Ezam. Ascend from Dane to Quin-archae, and then through the hierarchy to Archae to eventually transcend to Crystal Fold as Principae, and then to the Great Beyond.

Members of Dane
Thrisdane
Kydane (*kie-dane*)
Ashdane

DAIMON CASTE
Reside in any fold where angel caste has joined with other castes and produced offspring. The term is also used for those who have *any* angel caste heritage.

Moonsun Fold
Viv Wright

Wheel Fold
Anfarena – most senior (*an-far-reena*)
Anetherey (*a-neth-er-ray*)

HUMAN CASTE

Moonsun Fold
Members of Human Caste

Lettie Wright – Viv's mother
Jimmy (Ronald James) Wright – Lettie's husband
Rim (Rimmon) – gang leader

Wheel Fold
Scharii – travelling musicians (*shar-ree*)

Members of the Scharii
Tarchen en-Scharii (*tar-chen*)
Darch en-Scharii

About Wheel Fold: the eight sectors or Vales of Wheel Fold are: Eshavale, Ascavale, Warinavale, Genessavale, Beshavale, Terissavale, Sonoravale and Morvavale. These run north-south or cloudwise-starwise from the hub/peak: Astraal. The lake and city are also called Astraal.

Each Vale has countless smaller valleys or vals. Each Vale has a main river eg Eshavale - Eshacade; Ascavale - Ascacade etc. Settlements near the river take their name from the river eg Esh-embrin; Esh-accom. The tributaries flowing from the vals are rills. Smaller settlements (setts) take their name from the rills eg Scinta-ril. Inhabitants of these setts are identified by their sett: Ataghan en-Scinta-ril; Sehereden en-Scinta-ril.

Directions
Cloudwise – north
Starwise – south
Nightwise – west
Sunwise – east

Time Divisions
Zadicans (years) are divided by zadics of 45 days that include a period of recalibration in between (Vorash). Zadics are marked by constellations which appear and disappear in the night sky. Each has a particular meaning. The zadics are: Pool, Cascade, Fire, Ice, Lirium, Glimwing, Cadestone and Horse. Other brief zadics (Call Zadics), are meaningful to individuals and indicate the individual should visit the sacred city.

Eshavale – Vale of Wheel Fold
Members of the Eshadi
Ataghan en-Scinta-ril – Syld, band leader, lein to
Sehereden (*ata-gan*)
Sehereden en-Scinta-ril – lein to Ataghan, member of
Ataghan's band (*se-hera-den*)
'Poss' – a lost child found by Viv
Brithergen – member of Ataghan's band
Jethren – member of Ataghan's band
Anthran – member of Ataghan's band
Daran – member of Ataghan's band
Sandagh – member of Ataghan's band (*san-da*)
Inaghan – member of Ataghan's band (*in-a-gan*)

Eshadi Sylds (acknowledged leaders)
Ataghan en-Scinta-ril
Darthen en-Within-ril
Mathian en-Fessen-ril
Garath en-Moss-ril
Kurnen en-Vara-ril

Valen Setts (communities)

Tahsin's Sett
Tahsin – sett leader (*tar-sin*)
Enesha – harvester (*ee-nesh-a*)
Prenya – cook (*pren-ya*)
Borish – cook
Fahan – harvester – twin brother of Merhen (*fay-han*)
Merhen – harvester – twin brother of Fahan (*mer-han*)
Doran – guard, kitchen helper
Cazir – harvester, guard (*kaz-eer*)
Jered – harvester, guard

Amethen's Sett
Amethen – sett leader (*am-a-then*)
Drasen – band leader
Ithreya – sett member (*ith-ray-a*)

Stonash – a small people with hooded eyes, flattened faces and leathery skin - urrut traders
Long-arms – long-armed kin of the Stonash

LEFER CASTE

Wheel Fold
Lefer Caste are bird/bat-like beings with human caste-like intelligence

Members of Lefer Caste
Roaith en-Leferen – blue crest (*ro-aith*)
Garian en-Leferen – red crest – alpha of the Rookery.

BEASTMAN CASTE

Beastmen are puma-human mix creatures with human caste-like intelligence

IDIOMATIC EXPRESSIONS COMMON IN AUSTRALIA

Viv is Australian, and uses a range of idiomatic expressions.

Keep tabs on – check on; monitor
Didn't wash/did wash – didn't/did sound true; wasn't/ was acceptable

On the line – to take a risk/be at risk

Knocked-up – made pregnant; being pregnant

Get out of jail free card – from a board game where a special card grants the player advantages

Second chance draw – another ticket is picked out from the losing tickets in a lottery

Sticks the boots in – attacks physically or verbally

Dodged the honesty bullet – to 'dodge a bullet' is to escape something bad

Brownie points – points awarded by doing good deeds that will eventually grant a reward (from the junior group in the Girl Guides movement)

Take the cake – win the prize

Angel Caste Book 3
Angel Bone

Chapter 1

Viv struggled not to panic as she scanned the cavern. The gag made it hard to breathe, the rope cut her wrists and ankles, and the stone floor was cold. Her captor had been gone for a while giving her plenty of time to consider her predicament. Gettin' to be a bit of a habit, eh Vivi? Rim's goadings usually woke anger, but she was too frightened. Tarchen had been kind to Poss but now Poss was ill and alone and unless Viv escaped, she would stay that way.

The horse-riding bastard suspected Viv had mates she could shout for, which explained the gag and his sudden exit, unless he had gone to summon his mates. Here's our little friend who blew up our camp. Help yourselves! Sweat oozed down her back and she scanned again.

The bastard's pack was there but she was too tightly trussed to sit up, let alone search for a knife. And when he returned? She could expect rape but if it were rape and murder, or he took her with him, how long could Poss survive on her own? Two days? Three?

Poss might sleep off the fever and she had the food, but she would believe Viv had abandoned her and Viv's throat tightened. It did not matter what Poss thought of her as long as Poss survived!

There was only one more ridge to cross and Poss was smart. She had escaped the massacre *and* Viv when she had believed Viv was Waradi. Poss *could* reach Esh-accom on her own but there was third possibility Viv could hardly bear to think of: that ill and befuddled, Poss stumbled into her captor's clutches or those of the murderous thugs who destroyed her home.

Viv struggled to come up with a plan, but the harsh reality was she had nothing to trade. The man could take what he wanted from her body and beat the information he wanted from her head. Thris might be on his way back to rescue her, she thought wildly, but Rim's sarcasm crushed that hope. *Yep, Vivi. He'll arrive straight after the flying pigs.*

Footsteps rasped over the stone and Viv cringed as the man's hands wrenched her upright, dragged her back to the cave's entrance, and tore off the gag. His face held none of the mocking, gloating or sneering expressions of other sadistic bastards she had known but nor was it kind, and he looked like he had not slept for days.

Who *are* you?' he demanded.

'My name is Viv.'

He shook his head impatiently. '*What* are you? There's no sign of others. Are you alone?'

Viv made no response, unable to lie about Poss's existence, and his face hardened. 'Maybe I'm mistaken,' he muttered and wrenched her shirt open. Viv gasped but his attention was on her arm. 'Not even a scar,' he said in disgust, pulling her shirt roughly back into place. 'But it *was* you in the Leferen, wasn't it? And that means you're elddra.' Viv still could not speak. In his terms, she *was* elddra but she knew she was not.

'I can be a lot more persuasive if I have to,' he said harshly. 'And I don't have a lot of time.' He pushed his hand through his hair. 'Maybe I'll take you with me and we can speak as we go.'

'No!'

'Then answer me! What were you doing in the Leferen?'

'Looking for my mother.'

'In a gaming ring full of sap-suckers?' He smiled sourly. 'She's not likely to be in the middle of a burning camp either.'

'The gaming was cruel. I . . . I didn't mean to burn the camp. I … I just wanted a distraction so I could let the birdmen out.'

'Well, you certainly got one, not that the sap-suckers were grateful. And if my Waradi friends had caught you, a slashed arm would've been the least of your problems.' He winced as if injured but his interrogation continued. 'What were you going to steal just now?'

'Fire,' said Viv reluctantly.

'From my pack?' he said sarcastically.

'I needed a mug to carry coals in.'

'You were going to *steal* a mug to carry away fire coals when oilstone's all around us? Don't take me for a fool, elddra, *if* you want to live.' His dark eyes bored into hers then he took several paces away and Viv glanced at the walls. They looked perfectly ordinary.

'You'll travel with me,' he said, swinging back. 'At least until you remember what the truth looks like.'

'I'm telling the truth,' said Viv in panic. 'Please … I need to continue my journey.' She licked her lips. 'I'll give you whatever you want. Just let me go afterwards.'

'*Whatever I want*? You're shaking elddra, your offer as abhorrent to you as it is to me. Unlike some you might have come across, I only want the truth. Provide it and I'll consider letting you go.'

Viv nodded and the questions came thick and fast. Her full name, her Vale, her sett; any Sylds she knew; the men she had seen on her travels; burned settlements—where and how many; where she headed now, and why. The day drew on and Viv glanced worriedly at the light.

'You claim not to be of the Vales, but you wear Eshadi clothes,' the man said.

'I stole them.'

His lip curled. 'How long have you been a thief?'

'Since I was fourteen.'

'How old are you now?'

'Eighteen.'

'And why are you so anxious to be gone?'

'I have to get back—' began Viv and stopped.

'To the band that waits for you? Back to your murdering?'

'No! I'm not lying!'

'But you're not alone, are you?' he said softly. 'Who is it elddra? The Waradi lover whose bracelet you wear?'

'It's the bracelet from the gaming ring. You should recognise it. I … I kept it because it was pretty.'

He seized her arms and jerked her close. 'Tryst-bracelets aren't *pretty*, elddra. They're *binding*! It's time we left!'

'You promised to let me go!'

'Who—are—you—with?!' he snarled, his knife suddenly at her throat. 'Last chance, elddra!'

'I have a sick child,' she said wildly.

'Where?' Viv did not answer, and he unbound her feet. 'Take me to her now!' He dragged her along, his grip punishing as she stumbled over roots and through bushes until she stopped. 'If this is a trap ...' he hissed, knives ready as he stared about.

'She's *in* the tree,' said Viv.

He tethered her to the trunk and, with a final glare, clambered up through the branches. Silence stretched and Viv had started to fear what he was up to when he emerged from the foliage with Poss and the food slings. He lowered himself awkwardly to the ground, untethered Viv, and strode off with Poss.

He had no need to check she followed and by the time she struggled back up to the cave, made clumsy by her bound hands, he had rebuilt the fire and wrapped Poss in a blanket. Viv knelt beside her. 'Untie me,' she pleaded. 'You have my word I won't escape.'

'An elddra's word is worth less than spit in The Wheel,' he said, as he filled a pot with water. He settled it on the coals and rummaged in his pack. 'What have you given her?'

'Nothing.'

His head jerked round. 'Haven't you at least given her anamleaf?'

'I've got *nothing* to give her! Not even water!' Viv dropped her head and heard the clank of metal against metal as the man stirred something and it was a moment before he spoke again.

'What's the child named?'

'I don't know. I call her Poss.' Viv felt like crawling into a hole. Not only was she unable to give Poss the most basic of care, she had failed to earn enough trust to learn her name. She didn't *want* Poss to trust *anyone*, she reiterated fiercely. Trust opened the door to betrayal.

The quiet penetrated her seething thoughts and she looked up. The man cradled Poss in his lap and coaxed spoonfuls of liquid down her throat. His face was etched with weariness and rough with stubble, but his expression was tender. 'When you said you had a sick child, I though it might be yours. How did you come by her?' he asked.

'I found her,' said Viv and gave the barest outline of the crap-filled cavern, their journey to Poss's house, and their encounter with the Scharii.

'Esh-accom isn't the best place to head for,' he said.

'The Scharii said Poss might have family there,' said Viv, and wondered whether the Scharii had lied, or whether this man did.

'More than one band has breached the crests,' he said. 'Esh-accom might be safe, but the surrounding lands certainly aren't.' He winced as he slid Poss back into her bed of blankets, then rose and rebound Viv's ankles.

'The child should sleep the fever out and I must sleep too' he said and patted his knives. 'If you've lied to me and your Waradi or Ascadi friends do decide to visit, my first knife will be for her and my second one for you. You'll die knowing you've killed the child you love, elddra. Remember that.'

He wrapped himself in a blanket and was soon asleep leaving Viv to shiver and stew on her predicament. Since leaving home she had been a prisoner of the cat creature, the Scharii, and now this bastard. So much for the pleasant jaunt through the folds she had envisaged with Thris. She had been a prisoner at home too, she reminded herself, and not just of the Juvenile Detention Facility. Jimmy Wright's violence, the gangs, and loneliness had, in their own ways, all held her captive.

Men were easier to escape from than loneliness, she conceded. She had been shunned at school as the daughter of a drunk, then as a street-kid, and later as a criminal, then a *shekinah* and now as an *elddra*. Thris might dress up half-castes as one of the *uncountable possibilities of the Rynth*, but from what she had read in libraries, half-castes had never been welcome *anywhere*, at *any time* in history.

Chapter 2

By the time dawn crept back into the cave, Viv's misery had given way to anger. The bastard still slept snug in his blankets, but the fire had died, and she was frozen. She stared at the walls again and wondered if the mysterious oilstone really existed.

'Not happy this morning, elddra?' the man said, making her jump. He was propped on his elbow, his exhaustion of the previous night replaced with a sneer.

'I'm cold.'

The man shrugged out of his blankets and felt Poss's forehead. 'You'll have to excuse me for a moment,' he said, with mock politeness, and disappeared outside.

He had probably gone to pee, but had *she* needed to pee, she would have had to do it in her pants! His attitude had changed. Last night he had feared the violent company she might be keeping, but this morning he knew he was firmly in charge.

Viv was good at picking moods having spent her childhood working out Jimmy Wright's to avoid his fists *and* Rim's for the same reason, and she watched this man closely. Men did not fight alone, and she wondered whether his mates had been killed. He was wounded too, although he tried to hide it. Both things explained his attitude to her but not to Poss. Why heal the child of your enemies? Especially after you had killed the child's parents.

The man tossed a piece of stone into the coals, slammed his heel into it, and yellow flame blossomed. He tossed in more, topped up the fire with wood, and glanced sideways at her. 'I've heard that elddra aren't troubled by matters quarash. The needs of the body,' he added, as if she were a halfwit.

'You've kept me bound since yesterday,' said Viv, hoping it provided an explanation for her lack of peeing.

He crouched in front of her, and she flinched, but in the early morning light, he looked scarcely older than her. 'Fighting does that to you,' he said. 'It destroys settlements and people, but mostly it destroys trust. Those who could aid each other don't and so friends remain enemies.'

It was an odd thing to say but Viv was distracted by how dark his eyes were given his rusty brows and hair. Maybe the people here shared the same weird colour combinations as their horses. He continued to stare, and she scowled back. 'Should I trust you, elddra?' he asked.

'No,' she snapped.

He laughed softly. 'Not the answer I expected. Still, I don't want to be a completely *ungenerous* host,' he said and unbound her. 'If you need to attend to matters of quarash, you can do so at the back of the cave but if you do decide to take the air outside, I'll assume you're lost interest in the little girl's life.'

Viv's muscles were so cramped she struggled even to stand. She needed to harmonise to ease them but mainly to get her temper under control. She hobbled deeper into the cave, faced the wall and planted her feet wide. She would have liked to look out over the bright morning outside, but harmonising was hard enough without the bastard's threats.

She harmonised in the way Thris had taught her, relaxing each muscle in turn and slowing her breathing. Her head dropped forward and, as the tension drained from her body, her boiling thoughts subsided. It was easier

15

to visualise Thris in this state too, and she luxuriated in his perfection.

Birdcall roused her and she reluctantly opened her eyes. The man watched her from beyond the fire and she hoped he dismissed what he had seen as some weird elddra practice. She came back and knelt beside Poss relieved her sleep seemed normal.

'She needs another day of rest,' said the man, 'but I can delay no longer and that creates a problem.'

'We're no threat to you,' said Viv hurriedly. 'Let us go.'

'I agree the child's no threat,' he said. 'But you?' He shook his head. 'You know too much, elddra. You know where this cave is, and you know I'm wounded. You might not waste much breath in speech, but your eyes miss nothing. I'm taking you with me.' Viv stared at him in horror. 'I'll leave food and water for the child,' he continued, as he gathered his things. 'Esh-accom's less than three days away. She has a good chance of reaching it on her own.'

'Three days!' cried Viv, scrambling up. 'You said the lands around Esh-accom weren't safe. Let me go and I pledge to never speak of you, no matter what they do to me.'

'And if they threaten her?' he demanded, nodding at Poss. 'Would you speak then?'

Viv hesitated. 'She's only a child,' she said thickly. 'She deserves to be safe.'

There was a long silence while he considered her. 'Well answered, elddra,' he said finally. 'There's not much to trust about you but your dealings with the sap-suckers and the child tell me *something*.' He smiled grimly. 'It seems

I'm to gamble my life on the chance that trust between friends *can* be resurrected after all.

'I'll leave you *both* behind, elddra, but there's a price to pay,' he added and loomed closer. 'Swear never to speak of me unless you or the child are threatened with injury or death and *if* you do reach Esh-accom, pass on a message to the leader of the Eshadi Sylds.'

'But … that means I must speak of you,' said Viv in confusion.

'The Eshadi aren't my enemies.'

'But you're Waradi . . .'

'I'm not from that Vale either. Let's just say I had reason to visit.' His face filled with pain. 'The Waradi are even less generous hosts than me,' he continued hoarsely. 'If I hadn't been quick on my feet, I'd have suffered worse than a knife to the shoulder. They're not the kind to abandon a hunt either, elddra. Keep the child beyond their reach *and* yourself. They respect *nothing*.'

The man went west but Viv did not know whether he changed direction when he reached the trees, and nor did she care, too relieved he had gone. He left her his mug filled with the fever-reducing potion and a warning it would keep the child sleepy *and so delay their departure*, deduced Viv.

The man's generosity puzzled her, but she could neither delay nor carry the potion in an open mug, so she roused Poss enough to get the mixture into her then packed the mug away in one of the food pouches along with as much food as would fit. She needed to lighten her load given she must carry Poss but the second pouch created a problem. Burning it would leave fresh, *warm* ash, a sign to the man's pursuers someone had lately been there and so she stashed it in the darkest corner of the cave then set off, using her jacket as a sling for Poss again.

The man's warnings were stark in her head and she considered him as she climbed. He denied being Waradi so maybe he was some sort of spy, but for whose side? And who was fighting who anyway? And why? Viv was bound by her promise not to speak of him and yet to somehow deliver his message. *Enda lies nightwise.* What the hell did that mean?

Was *enda* a person or a place? And *lies* a position or deceit? And given that north seemed to be cloudwise, east sunwise and south starwise, did *nightwise* mean west, or was it simply some shitty connotation of darkness? She might not be able to pass on the message anyway. She had no idea what a *syld* was and had no intention of hanging around Esh-accom to find out. An *elddra* was unlikely to be welcomed anyway and there was no way she was going to be held prisoner again.

Chapter 3

Poss woke as the light ebbed but Viv did not pause, driven on by the ice-edged wind and the need to get the endless trek over with. She was so high she could see the peak she had first glimpsed when she fled the birdmen. Its gleam reminded her of the White Helixai but the peak's lower slopes were wreathed in cloud. She wondered whether the cloud was permanent, like the mist where she had found Thris again, and her hands clenched as the ache of longing roused. They *would* be together again, she told herself, for the umpteenth time.

The wind's bluster made the climb harder and when she reached a jut of stone, she collapsed in its lee and cradled Poss on her lap. Her shirt was soaked with sweat, and her shoulders ached, but Poss's closeness was comforting, and she cuddled her as the wind shrieked about them.

'I used to be frightened of the asht-winds,' murmured Poss. 'Then da told me it was just the asht-sprites, squealing in excitement as they rode the winds down from Astraal. You don't have to carry me anymore,' she added and planted a warm kiss on Viv's cheek. 'You've carried me all the way from the last ridge.'

'I rested in a cave for a while,' said Viv, moved by the kiss. 'I wasn't walking all the time.'

'You need your jacket anyway,' said Poss, which was true. Viv put it on and adjusted the belt on Poss's jacket to make sure she was snug.

The wind continued to shriek, and Viv hauled herself up. 'We need to keep moving,' she said. 'Hold tight to my hand. I don't want you being carried away by any asht-sprites. We'll find some shelter for a proper rest further up.'

'If this is the ridge next to Soaich's Spine, there's no shelter until the rill. Da says the ridge caught its nastiness from its neighbour,' added Poss darkly.

Viv barely heard her, too busy calculating the risks of continuing down the ridge's other side in the dark but when they reached the ridge top Poss was too tired to go on anyway. There was no shelter, as Poss had warned, and Viv found a shallow overhang and scooped out loose stone to make a crude nest. With Poss curled in her arms, it was actually quite snug.

Poss was soon asleep and astonishingly, Viv felt her own eyelids droop and drowsily kissed the top of Poss's head. *Feelin' sentimental, are ya, Vivi?* In truth, she was. It might be one of her last nights with the little girl and if it were, it meant Poss was safe, and that was all that mattered.

Viv was woken by rain. It was still dark, and she pulled her jacket over Poss, but water seeped into their hollow and she had to rouse Poss. The wind had dropped but it was cold, and Viv glanced at Poss anxiously fearing she might sicken again.

Viv had no idea whether it was closer to midnight or closer to dawn, but the lack of shelter meant they had to go on. She took Poss's hand and started down the slope. Viv had excellent night vision, which had proved handy when thieving at night, but she snatched glances towards the east in the hope of some sign of dawn.

Poss went without complaint and Viv wondered if she had inherited her stoic streak from her da. The little girl was nothing like the children at the squats, who grizzled all day. Even so, their progress was slow, and they still had the last ridge to cross. At least the final part of the journey *down* a valley should be speedier.

Her thoughts turned to Esh-accom. For some reason, she imagined it as a medieval town, with a wall and Tudor-style buildings, but given Ezam's angels lived in buildings in the style of Ancient Greece, and Hearth Fold's Keeper in a biscuit-tin lid cottage, it could be anything.

The burned settlements had been just a few houses but Darch had given the impression Esh-accom was bigger. Presuming Poss's da still lived, as Darch implied, he might have gone to Esh-accom to summon fighters. It fitted with him having sent Poss to another settlement, although that had proved a mistake.

Darch had warned that Poss's da was dangerous and Viv chewed on her lip as she considered his failure to protect his daughter. Dangerous *and* stupid was never a good combination. Hopefully, she would not have to meet him. *Hopefully*, she would deliver Poss to the gate *if* there were a gate, and someone would know where to take her, or Poss would know where to go. The Scharii's dislike of elddra had been clear as had the horse-riding bastard's although Viv sensed his behaviour partly stemmed from being hunted and hurt.

Even so, there was a hell of a lot about him that made no sense. He denied being Waradi yet looked like the men at the camp *and* had chased her afterwards. Maybe he had fallen out with his Waradi mates or maybe he was hunted by Poss's people, although that made no sense either. Why insist Viv pass on a message to an Eshadi *Syld*, unless it was some sort of insult.

21

'You're thinking bad things again, aren't you?' said Poss.

'What?'

'When you look like that, you're thinking bad things. I want you to stay with me at Esh-accom, Viv, where you'll be safe.'

'I need to continue my journey, Poss. Besides, you won't need me anymore. Your da will be there and other people who love you.' Viv forced a smile. 'You'll have fun with all the other children.'

'Da might be dead and I don't want *them*. I want you.'

Viv could think of nothing to say. Poss's grasp on reality belonged to someone twice her age. Da might indeed be dead and, to make matters worse, Viv had only considered her own feelings at losing Poss, not Poss's feelings at losing her.

She crouched so her face was level with the little girl's. There was so much she wanted to tell her, but dare not, for both their sakes. 'I was looking for my mother when I found you, Poss. As soon as you're safe, I must continue my search.'

'But you don't *need* a mother if you've got a choose- or seed-father!' cried Poss, close to tears.

'My arsehole of a choose-father is dead, and my seed-father is a shit,' said Viv bluntly.

'What is *arsholl* and *asshit*?'

'*Shit* is what comes out of your *arse hole* during matters of quarash,' said Viv briefly, regretting she had taught Poss bad language. Poss opened her mouth to respond but Viv cut her off. 'We need to keep moving,' she said and Poss's lip trembled, making Viv feel like *she* was the arsehole.

The rain eased, and fog took its place, but it was silvery, as if somewhere to the east or *sunwise*, dawn had broken. They were both wet but Poss's hand was warm in hers and Viv's mood lifted. She expected to see bushes and trees again as they descended, but the ridge's lower slopes were as barren as its crest. 'Why doesn't anything grow here?' she asked.

'Why should it?'

'The other Vales had trees and bushes,' muttered Viv, tripped up by her assumptions *again*. If gold and silver trees with metallic leaves grew in Ezam *where it never rained*, then it was perfectly reasonable nothing grew here where it did.

'They're vals not Vales,' corrected Poss with a sigh. 'I don't understand why you don't know what everyone else does. Is it because your seed-father was a shit?'

'It's best not to use that word,' said Viv. 'It's not very nice.' Hell! She sounded like her own mother.

'Is it because of your seed-father?' pursued Poss.

'Possibly,' said Viv and braced for questions about her parentage.

'It's not your fault your seed-father was Astraali,' said Poss indignantly. 'Da won't blame you for something that's not your fault. He'll let you stay with us.'

'Everyone seems to hate the elddra except you,' said Viv, attempting to make light of it.

'Don't take any notice of the Scharii,' said Poss. 'Da says they're jealous because the Astraali keep the best music-makers for themselves.'

'They're not the only ones who hate . . .' began Viv and stopped as she recalled Poss had slept through the encounter with the man in the cave. The little girl did not seem to notice Viv's sudden lack of speech, her brow wrinkled in thought. She looked so serious Viv playfully flicked a drip of water from her chin. 'Whatch-ya thinkin', Possy?'

Poss stopped and her dark eyes came to Viv's. 'Will you be my lein?'

Viv's mind raced. If a lein-tryst was akin to marriage, being a lein must be pretty serious too. 'I can't stay with you, Poss,' she said gently.

'It doesn't mean you have to stay with me. It means you'll always be part of me, no matter where you are, and I'll always be part of you.'

'Your da might not like it.'

'It's a choice for each Valen to make or not to make,' said Poss with quiet dignity.

'Don't you have to be over a certain age?' *Like eighteen*? Poss shook her head and Viv glanced around uneasily. The fog was thinning, and the growing light made it easier to see *and be seen*. 'How is it done?' she asked quickly.

'We swear it,' said Poss and held up her right hand. Viv reluctantly followed suit and Poss's small fingers linked through hers. 'I, Fariye, claim Violet Iris Vacia as my lein. She is me and I am her.'

Poss looked at Viv expectantly and Viv collected her scattered wits. 'I, Violet Iris Vacia, claim Fariye as my lein. She is me and I am her.'

Poss smiled tremulously and kissed Viv on each cheek, and Viv kissed her back, but she felt numb. Poss had revealed her name but the act of trust was not all that rocked Viv. For the first time in her life, someone had chosen her, *permanently*. There were no threats, no trade-offs, no blackmail. *She is me and I am her*. End of story.

Chapter 4

Thris had no time to test the rift's resonance, the tusked-creature almost on them, but as he hurtled down the iridescent tunnel with Ky, he knew it did not exit in Ezam, and when he finally stepped from it, he simply stared. Rectangular slabs of black stone stretched away in every direction, their gleaming planes as smooth as glass, and their narrow passages reminiscent of the Bokos's labyrinthine ways.

Their oddness distracted Ky and Thris shifted his grip to his hand. 'What *is* this fold?' whispered Ky.

'I have not read of it,' said Thris.

'They are like the Black Obsidian Stele and there are *hundreds* of them,' said Ky, fear creeping back into his voice.

'I sense no threat,' said Thris soothingly. 'If they tested us like the Black Obsidian Stele, we would have felt it by now. I think their resemblance is coincidental.'

Ky's eyes darted this way and that. 'I do not want to stay here,' he said. 'Is the rift still open?' It was too dangerous to return to the previous fold, but Thris sensed for the rift to placate Ky. It had closed but a faint resonance perfumed the air and his heart missed. Viv had been in there!

'Is the rift still open?' repeated Ky.

'No,' said Thris distractedly.

'But …what if there is no other rift? What if we are marooned?'

'The Tome tells us folds with rifts in, have rifts out,' said Thris, forcing his attention back to Ky The Tome also said it could be eons before they opened. 'Let us go on.'

'Which way?'

It was a good question. The passages ran away from them in all directions. It was like a hedge maze Thris had once visited in Moonsun. Human caste delighted in finding their way through a series of blocked passages to a central point and then back again. It had seemed pointless, but he wished he had paid more attention to their strategies.

No resonance flowed from the passageways and he decided to reconnoitre from the air. Rifts were only found at ground level, but he wanted to see if the stone slabs were an anomaly they had exited the rift into by chance. He shared his thoughts with Ky and they launched skywards, but were less than halfway up the slabs' sides when a green mist formed above them. Ky hesitated but Thris continued skywards and then, without warning, the mist transformed into writhing spectral shapes.

Ky shrieked and dived back to the stone floor but Thris descended more slowly, his gaze on the apparitions, and when they dissolved back into the mist, he flew skywards again. The effect was immediate and a lot more violent. The wraiths lunged at him with teeth and claws, and the air temperature plummeted, cramping his wings so that he landed awkwardly.

'What are they?' whispered Ky, his horrified gaze on the remnant green wisps.

'Some human caste folds tell of *ghosts*,' said Thris slowly. 'The essence of dead human caste that failed to reach the Great Beyond. Some ghosts are pitiable, but others taunt the living. I do not know whether these are ghosts, but they guard the heights which means we must stay on the ground.'

The passages looked identical so they chose one at random and set off. The stone swallowed the sound of their footsteps, so that it seemed they walked in a vacuum, and they had not gone far before stone blocked the way and they retraced their steps. The second passage had other passages that ran off it but all of them, including the one they followed, ended in stone and again they returned to their starting point.

The third passage seemed more promising, with a greater choice of turnings, but they still had to back-track more than once, having to rely on their memories of the way. Had Thris been in Ezam, he would have used his and Ky's resonant prints to retrace their steps, but the stone swallowed resonance too and Thris found its absence distressing. It was as if nothing here had ever lived.

The silvery light remained even and while it prevented them from colliding with walls, it was useless as a navigation aid. They went on along the third passageway's twists and turns and were a long way into the last unblocked passage, when it too ended.

Thris stared as the smooth black stone that confronted them. 'I am not sure I can find my way back,' he admitted.

'I have memorised the turns *and* counted our steps to keep my mind off the wraiths,' said Ky with a shaky smile.

Counting steps and memorising turns was an obvious thing to do but Thris's mind had become curiously blank. 'Can you find our way back?' he asked.

'I think so.'

Thris wondered whether Ky's confidence was misplaced but he matched his steps to Ky's and after a long trek through the undifferentiated stone, and numerous turns, they arrived at their starting point. 'That was well done,' he said in relief. 'Are you able to do it again?'

'Of course,' said Ky, with a smile reminiscent of their tussles in the trials.

They set off again and while each new passage seemed longer and more complex than the last, all ended in stone, and Ky brought them safely back until only one passage remained to be tried.

They rested and Thris attempted to harmonise and failed, something that had not happened since he was a new Dane. The fold's lack of resonance might be to blame or something else. The passages' increasing complexity was unlikely to be random and he wondered whether the slabs acted like the Blue Helixai, shifting after he and Ky had passed, with rifts opening in passages they had already tried.

'What will we do if the last passage goes nowhere?' asked Ky.

'I do not know,' said Thris and instantly regretted his candour but Ky looked more thoughtful than fearful.

'That is the first time I have heard you admit you do not know what to do.'

'That was true of before . . .' Thris trailed off, still finding it hard to speak of his time with the Principae.

'I want things to be like they were *before* the shekinah,' said Ky fiercely. 'Just you and me and Ash. It was enough, was it not, Thris? Just the three of us?'

'It was enough to be happy but not enough to ascend,' said Thris slowly and wondered suddenly whether his failed Guideship served a greater purpose than to reveal his flaws. Perhaps confronting his fallibility was a lesson in itself and his predicament not an *aberration* from the path to ascendance but the actual path! It would explain why his sexual encounter with Viv had healed rather than harmed him.

Or maybe his ruminations confirmed his continuing arrogance! Hope dimmed but was not entirely snuffed out. The Great Beyond might have ordained he end his days here, but he was with an angel he loved, and who loved him, and that love was worth fighting for. 'Ready to count?' he asked. Ky nodded and they embraced, then set off down the last of the passageways.

Chapter 5

The fog had cleared by the time Viv reached the valley floor to reveal a bright, sunshiny day. The blue sky and warmth reminded her of spring, except there was nothing green in sight, the soaring slope of the next ridge as barren as the one they had descended.

The valley might be stony, but it had water: a fast-flowing rill, crystal clear and cold enough to be meltwater. They drank and Viv peered up at the next ridge. It was enormous. Just her luck it lay between them and the last, *easiest*, part of their trek.

'I think that's Soaich's Spine,' said Poss following her gaze. 'Da says only the cleverest Eshadi horses can cross it.'

Viv glanced down at Poss, no, at *Fariye*. She practised it silently, *Far-ree-ay*, and wonder at being granted the child's trust washed over her afresh followed by worry the name might identify her as someone important. It would be safer to call her Poss at least until they reached Esh-accom.

'If that is Soaich's Spine, then this is the Dart Rill,' continued Poss.

'Have you been here before?'

'I can't remember. I might have with da when he took me to Esh-accom for the tournaments.'

Viv had no idea what sort of tournaments the fold might hold but crossing the ridge was a more pressing problem, even if it were called a *spine*. 'We'd better make a start. At least the weather's nice,' she added.

'It changes quickly on Soaich's Spine,' said Poss.

'More reason to get going then,' said Viv with forced cheerfulness. They found a place where stones formed a crossing and then started to climb. Viv was careful to have regular rest stops and made sure Poss ate and drank, and Viv sipped water, but the climb was as hard as she feared. There were whole sections where gravel slipped away and where broken rock broke again as they picked their way across.

The weather remained fine, but it was very quiet, and the silence made Viv uneasy. 'Don't leaf-lilters come here?' she asked. 'Or ridge-roosters?' she added, dredging up another bird name.

'There's no scharii,' said Poss dismissively.

Viv had no idea what the musicians had to do with the lack of birds and her confusion must have been plain because Poss suppressed a sigh, obviously trying to be patient with her *lein*. 'The leaf-lilters eat the scharii on the brevis and acanth bushes, and brevis and acanth bushes don't grow here,' she explained.

'But why are they called the same as the musicians?' asked Viv, curiosity getting the better of her.

'Because of the *yu-angar*,' said Poss. 'You saw them play it,' she added.

'Oh,' said Viv, as she recalled the shield-shaped drum.

'The scharii have wings like the yu-angar the Scharii play,' said Poss and smirked. 'Da says the Scharii think they're too important to share their name with a leaf-eater but if they were that special, they would be allowed to stay in the Astraali city.'

It was past midday before they struggled the last of the way to the crest, but they did not delay there long. The

31

crest was narrow, and sharp with shattered stone, and Viv saw why it was called Soaich's *Spine* although *Dinosaur Spine* would have fitted too. She was keen to reach the valley before dark, find somewhere sheltered for Poss to have a good, long sleep, and then start off fresh in the morning for the final part of their journey.

The weather stayed fine and the sky birdless, and neither Viv nor Poss broke the quiet with chatter. They had to concentrate on every step, the descent as inhospitable as the climb. Viv had a good head for heights and was sure-footed, and it turned out Poss shared the same traits. She would make a good burglar, Viv mused, as they made their way down, but Viv would not wish that life on anyone, least of all a child.

They reached the valley floor without incident and found a nice snug over-hang to shelter under for the night. Viv should have felt relieved, but things were going a bit too smoothly and she had never enjoyed much luck. She was not hungry but ate to placate Poss who seemed to think Viv starved herself for Poss's sake. 'Leins share *everything*,' Poss told her.

The little girl was soon asleep, but Viv remained propped against the stone, her gaze on the valley. Unlike the other valleys, this one was broad, and while she could not see the rill, she could hear its rush.

Thirin Rill, Poss had called it, and the earlier one had been *Dart Rill*. Stream in the Dart valley, and stream in the Thirin valley, she mused. There was a logic to the naming system that made sense *once* you got the hang of it. One thing she had *not* got the hang of was the constellations or *zadics* that appeared to make the sky as bright as day and then disappeared with equal speed. So far in the Rynth she had encountered cat creatures and suffocating sandstorms but also things of beauty like the red, green, and yellow stars of the cat creatures' fold, and the constellations here.

She supposed all folds held beauty and ugliness because before she had lived in the gangs' dingy squats and stinking alleys, she had perched in gums and watched the owls' dark swoop against the glitter of the Milky Way. She just hoped there was more beauty than ugliness in the fold where her mother lived.

The new day was full of golden light like autumn, Viv's favourite season, and she hoped it was a good omen. The valley was promising too. The others had been narrow and rocky, but this one was broad with a smooth swathe of river-sand that made their travel easier. 'It's very different to the Dart Rill,' she said to Poss, as they breakfasted.

'*Enda* gives when *Soaich* takes.'

Enda had been part of the man in the cave's message. *Enda lies nightwise.* The odds were shortening *Enda* was some sort of god and that *Soaich* as well, and it was easy to guess which was the good guy and which the bad. Viv peered up at the rocky spur behind them. They had done well to climb it *and* safely make it down into the valley.

Poss's chattiness increased as they trekked along the sand and Viv learned Esh-accom did indeed have a wall and there were other big, *walled*, settlements in Eshavale too. Sometimes the urrut were taken to Esh-accom to be collected by the *Stonash*, and other times the *Stonash* came to the *setts* to get them. The *Stonash* went everywhere, even through the Grey Fire, and right up to the Astraali city.

33

Poss was full of useful information that Viv filed away. From what Poss had said earlier, Viv knew her da grazed urrut and that the Stonash were probably traders. She had no idea what the Grey Fire was but learned Poss's da had a *compound* at Esh-accom *and* sett members, and that he always won the tournaments. There would be tournaments soon, Poss told her excitedly, and Viv would have fun in Esh-accom, especially during Fire Zadic.

Viv let her rattle on and not just because Viv needed to know as much as possible about the fold. For the first time in their travels together, Poss sounded like a normal, happy little girl who occasionally and shyly, now called Viv *lein*.

While the river-sand made for an easy walk, its smooth sweep broken only by the occasional trunk washed down in the last flood, it provided no hiding places. It would be safer to scramble along in the bushes part-way up the valley's sides but a hell of a lot slower and Viv just wanted the journey to end.

The flocks of yellow birds that fed on something in the sand provided a type of warning system by rising in squawking clouds at their approach and settling again behind them. According to Poss they were *thirin* and lived only in this val. Her da said Enda smiled on them because *they knew where they belonged and were content there*. The words resonated but Viv knew that things in real life were seldom that simple.

Chapter 6

Viv grew more appreciative of the thirin as the day wore on and the rill elbowed around rocky spurs that obscured the way ahead and behind. Poss searched the sand for the birds' buttery-yellow feathers as they walked and discarded those she collected earlier in favour of brighter or shapelier ones. She had always collected feathers, she confided, and had over fifty before da sent her to Esh-embrin.

She fell silent and Viv stopped near a large tree trunk. 'Time for lunch,' she said cheerfully. 'And our chairs await.' They perched on the trunk, smoothed from its roll down the river, and Viv pulled food from the pouch, careful to leave the mug at the bottom. If worse came to worse, what Poss did not know, could not be forced from her.

'Do you—' she began. Thirin squawks erupted from the bend in front and then the unmistakable sound of galloping horses. There was no time to unbed her wings or run and Viv frantically gouged sand from against the trunk, grabbed Poss and the food pouch, and thrust them into the narrow trench. 'Keep your face to the trunk for air and no matter what happens, *stay there*!' she ordered as she shovelled the sand back.

'Viv!' cried Poss in terror.

'If you love me, *lein*, stay there!' hissed Viv, then sprinted to the water's edge and dropped to her knees as if she drank, but all she did was pray. *Please God, please God, let the horses be grey with silver manes and tails*! The first of the riders galloped into view and Viv's breath emptied. The horses were dark with a rusty manes and tails.

She fled along the sand, using every technique Thris had taught her, and her speed and endurance were phenomenal. The longer they took to catch her, the further they were from Poss, but catch her they would. Their shouts filled the valley as they ran her to ground and as the lead horse's breath hit the back of her neck, Viv threw herself sideways into the rill.

Its rider drove his horse in after her and she ducked under its neck, got a grip on the stone on the opposite bank, and scrabbled up. And then she was seized from behind. He wrenched her around and she glimpsed the blaze of his yellowy eyes before he grabbed her by the hair and smashed her head back against the stone.

There was a crack, an explosion of pain, and the world receded. She was dimly aware he had wrenched the tryst-bracelet from her wrist, held it aloft, and shouted. Only his voice rang out, the other men silent as he shoved the bracelet back on her wrist and yanked down her pants. His breath was sour and she turned her face away and stared skywards at the yellow birds that wheeled as bright as angels against the blue, and then he slammed into her.

Viv's breath burst from her lungs and she tried to drag in more as he pulled back and slammed into her again and again. His body held her crushed against the stone and then the tension drained from him, as the hot liquid drained from her, down her shaking legs.

He smiled at her then, almost tenderly as he lifted a wet curl from her face, but Viv could scarcely stand, pain from the rape and the crack to her head pounding through her in nauseating waves. He hauled her back across the rill and onto his horse, then vaulted on behind and they were galloping again. She slumped back against him, too ill to sit upright, and he held her in place, his hand under her shirt as he pawed at her breasts.

Viv yearned to escape into unconsciousness, but the rats of memory slashed at her with flashbacks of every violent assault she had endured. She fought to blunt their wounds with the understanding that Poss was safe but Poss was not safe. She was a little girl lost and a lein lost to Viv forever.

Time seemed to jag, and she became aware that some of the horses were riderless. There must have been a fight at some point earlier, she concluded groggily, and the men's speed the result of pursuit. Hope flared it was the Eshadi and she and Poss were to be rescued, but she had never been rescued by anybody. All she had to hold onto was that the rapist seemed to be the leader and so unlikely to share his prize at least until it was expedient.

She managed to crank her head up. The valley had narrowed, the rill a rush of water to her right, the sheer sides of Soaich's Spine soaring to her left. One of the men shouted and her captor wrenched his horse to a halt. The other horses milled about them as an argument broke out and then one of the riders exclaimed and pointed upwards.

There was a horseman there, high on Soaich's Spine, and silence fell but then her captor gestured crudely in the horseman's direction. He was right to be unconcerned. By the time the horseman made it down, *if* he did, the men would be long gone. And then two things happened at once: the sound of galloping erupted ahead, and the horseman above jumped down the cliff. The horse landed on a ledge, paused, and jumped again. It jumped like a cat, as the man in the cave's had during the pig-bear attack.

There were other horsemen on the cliff now, jumping down the sheer stone, but any new hope of rescue died. The horses' dark manes and tails told her they were not Eshadi either but nor did they appear to be the Waradi's friends and any semblance of order disintegrated.

Her captor bawled commands but as horsemen appeared ahead, some of his men abandoned their mounts and fought their way through the rill's rush to the cover on the other side. Others wrenched their mounts around and galloped back the way they had come. Her captor did neither. He jagged his heels into his horse's sides and drove it up Soaich's Spine.

Blood sprayed from its nostrils, but it managed to reach a ledge and her captor leapt off, dragged off Viv, and crouched behind it. Below them, men fought with knives and Waradi fell, their deaths strangely silent in a battle without guns. And then, the scene below was obliterated, as a massive horse jumped from above and landed in front of them.

Her captor had an instant to save himself and he used it. He drove his booted heels into the legs of his mount and sent it sprawling into the legs of their attacker's mount. The attacker's horse jumped backwards to avoid the impact, but the ledge was narrow, and it was forced to leap to lower ground.

Viv's captor grabbed her jaw and wrenched her face to his. 'I *own* you, *lein-tryst*, remember that!' he snarled, and then he was off between the slabs of broken stone with a speed that belied his bulk.

Viv's brain told her to run too but she lacked the strength even to stand and then the attacker leapt back onto the ledge and his knife flashed towards her heart. And stopped. There was another man there now, his hand clamped about her attacker's wrist. 'Not *this* time, lein,' the second man said. 'We're not as they are.'

The blade remained poised as if the men's strength were equal, then disappeared as her attacker shifted his grip to her arm. He felt the tryst-bracelet and his teeth flashed in a savage smile as he wrenched it off. 'Not *yet*, Sehereden,' he corrected, and dragged her down the slope.

Chapter 7

Nothing could have prepared Viv for the carnage below. She had seen war footage on the news, but it had not shown severed fingers, or the bloody snail-trails corpses made when dragged towards a pyre. Viv staggered and her captor grunted impatiently. 'Take her, Sehereden, while I finish up here,' he said.

Viv felt herself transferred to the other man, but her legs gave way, and he brought his arm around her waist. His touch woke the horror of the rape and she screamed, then her vision blacked, and she was on the grass, vomiting until bile scoured her throat.

The man crouched beside her then pressed something to her lips. 'Drink this,' he ordered, and Viv gulped convulsively. Whatever it was burned all the way down and returned the world to focus. The man, *Sehereden*, had the same black hair, dark eyes, and handsome chiselled features as Rim, but his blood-soaked jacket reminded Viv of what he really was, of what they *all* were.

'What are you named, elddra?' he asked.

'Viv.'

'Short for Vivreya?'

'No.'

'Why were you with the Waradi?'

'I'll tell you why she was with the Waradi *leader*,' said the first man, appearing in Viv's line of vision. He held the bracelet aloft. 'She travelled with her lein-tryst, helped him with his murderous work, *comforted* him afterwards. I've left the pyre unlit, Sehereden. We've another body to add, two in fact, but her lover's kept his filthy skin intact a while longer.' He pulled a knife from his belt. 'Will you do the honours, lein, or shall I?'

Viv found it hard to breathe. If only she had not kept the bracelet! It had damned her before and it damned her now, but then she realised tossing the bracelet away would not have saved her. War had nothing to do with justice.

Sehereden's expression had hardened, but at least he looked rational, unlike the first man. They looked similar enough to be brothers, but the first man had a lot more in common with Rim. Viv did not know what he chewed, snorted or smoked, but he was tanked on it. It was there in the jar of his movements, the jagged pattern of his speech, in the way he held himself even at rest. And like Rim, he was on the edge of violence, and in a bizarre parody of her old life, she was to be the trigger.

'If she's the Waradi leader's lein-tryst, there's much she can tell us about him *and* them,' said Sehereden.

'I've no time for lies,' the first man clipped out.

'I don't lie,' whispered Viv.

The man thrust his face close, and she recoiled, the drug more potent up close. 'Is the Waradi leader your lein-tryst?' he demanded.

'No.'

'I can *smell* him on you!' He smiled mockingly. 'Was it good?' he asked softy. 'His pleasuring of you? Did it make you hungry for more? Is that why you followed him here? To feel him hard inside you, night after night, after he'd finished his killing?'

His words were as lethal as his knives, but Viv knew the game he played. The gangs were experts at it, and she had learned its rules too: show no fear, fear was weakness, weakness was death. She forced herself to hold his gaze. 'Does *imagining* it give *you* pleasure, arsehole?' she asked, and braced for a blow, but there was a burst of heat instead, and she glanced at the pyre in confusion thinking it had been lit.

The man swung away, and she saw his muscles bunch and ripple under his jacket. Whatever crap he was on played havoc with his body. Sehereden watched him too. *Lein*, the first man had called him. Leins were part of each other, Poss had said, and that left little room for disagreements. It was clear who was the boss too.

The leinship might have stopped the man from killing her immediately, but it would not delay her murder much longer. It was quiet, the only sound the rush of the rill, and knowing these were to be her last moments of life, she looked away from the men and corpses, and up to the sky. It was silvered with dusk, but dawn was her favourite time, when light chased away darkness. She gripped the feather at her neck. It was strange but comforting Thris would be here with her at the end of everything and then, inexplicably, she heard bells.

The men who waited near the corpses heard them too and turned. 'Light the pyre!' the first man ordered, and they leapt into action, smashing rocks under booted-heels and tossing them onto the heap. The wood caught first, followed by the clothing, and then the smoke blackened as the flames found fat.

The man grabbed Viv's arm and hauled her upright, but his gaze was on Sehereden. 'It seems our problems are solved, lein,' he said, and dragged her towards the fire. Every picture Viv had ever seen of witch-burnings smashed back and she kicked and clawed at him with all her strength. Sehereden followed, his face expressionless.

'Our Waradi lein-tryst doesn't like the heat,' the man grunted, as he wrestled her forward. 'Which is just as well, given she's to return to her maker.'

'You're sending her with the Stonash?'

'*You* won't have her killed, lein, and *I* won't have her left. She'll travel the crests, back to the cloud-crawlers who seeded her.'

'She won't survive the journey.'

'Why not, lein? Every Valen knows the elddra do not suffer as we do.' He twisted Viv's arm up her back and as she shrieked and doubled over in pain, wrenched the feather from her neck, and dangled it before her eyes. 'You'll go into death without your amé to guide you,' he said harshly. 'See it as a reward for those you've sent on ahead of you.' And with that, he threw the feather into the fire.

Viv's scream was so primal that those who watched clutched their own amés. She was aware of being dragged away from the fire's heat, but of little else. Pain consumed her, not just the physical pain of her injuries, but something more profound, as if the very core of her had been wounded. The man continued to haul her along, but Viv no longer struggled, lost in a world empty of hope.

River-sand gritted under her feet and then grass and, as the sound of bells grew louder, she managed to raise her head. Creatures like cattle appeared but they were twice the size with mustard-coloured fleece that hung in ringlets to the ground and great sweeping horns like the handlebars of gigantic bikes. They came slowly, tethered side by side to a single rope, the bells at their necks chiming with every step.

The creatures were so strange it took Viv time to notice their herders. They were small folk with hoods drawn low, but as they neared, she saw their flat-featured faces and long arms. Monkey-dwarves! Viv fought to free herself and the man's grip became punishing. 'Take her,' he ordered Sehereden, and went forward to meet the monkey-dwarves.

Sehereden's grip was kinder, but no less firm. 'Neither the urrut nor Stonash will harm you,' he said.

One of the monkey-dwarves had drawn off with the man but their conversation did not last long before the man handed something over and they spat to seal some sort of deal, then the man strode back with a collar like the urrut wore, but smaller, and with a leash attached. Viv strained away from him as he fastened it around her neck, and she heard two clicks, then he used the leash to drag her towards the urrut.

He could have taken her arm, but he wanted to humiliate her, and Viv screwed her head around and made eye contact with Sehereden. He had shown some semblance of kindness, but his face was impassive, and Viv reminded herself underlings never challenged their leaders. The man fastened the leash to the end of the tether rope and Viv heard the clicks again. Up close, the urrut were immense, and she backed away as far as the leash allowed.

'Enjoy your journey, elddra,' the man sneered.

'My name's Viv, arsehole!' retorted Viv. 'Violet, Iris, Vacia. Viv.' The man's contemptuous expression remained unchanged, and he strode back to Sehereden and they moved off together. Neither looked back.

Viv yanked at the collar. The arsehole pretended she was less than human to justify killing her! *She won't survive the journey*, Sehereden had said. She bloody well *would* survive it, if only to spite them! Picking locks was her stock in trade and once she was free, she would be off down the nearest rift, *wherever* it led!

Monkey-dwarves appeared around the side of the urrut, and Viv's anger swung back to fear. *Stonash*, not monkey-dwarves, she corrected, noting their shorter arms, but they had to be close kin. Whatever they were, they ignored her, just prodded an urrut up that had lain down before they disappeared back to the front of the line. Then a horn sounded, and the urrut lumbered forward, dragging Viv with them.

Ataghan glanced at Sehereden as they made their way back to the pyre. It was all but dark, but he had no need of light to know his lein's feelings. The fire burned fiercely, the air full of the smell of roasting meat. Humans and animals smelled the same once the flames got to them, and Ataghan had eaten no meat since the killing began.

'I'm heading cloudwise,' he said shortly. 'There's another body to add to the pyre. I'll understand if you choose to return to Esh-accom with the men.'

'I hunt with you, Syld.'

Sehereden kept his anger to himself but knowing it was there, riled Ataghan. 'You think we should let those live who murder their way through our Vale?'

'Those from Esh-min who rode with us certainly don't,' said Sehereden, his gaze on the mutilated corpses. 'But I begin to wonder, Syld, where the line now is that divides us from our enemies.'

'I know you've long had a preference for *blue* eyes, *lein*, but the elddra wore Eshadi clothes and, as I'm sure you noticed, they were from *my* val!'

Sehereden's eyes flashed in the firelight. 'Valen-lore prohibits the harming of women!'

'*And* the old *and* the young. Tell that to those of Eshembrin!' Ataghan strode away and Sehereden heard him bawl orders to the waiting men then whistle Taris.

The fire flared as the corpses settled and something gleamed at the fire's edge. It was the tryst- bracelet and on an impulse, Sehereden hooked it out with his boot and juggled the hot metal into his pocket. Then he whistled Fara, leapt onto his back, and followed his lein into the darkness.

Chapter 8

Thris and Ky moved steadily along the passageway between the black stones. They exchanged no words and Ky counted no steps. Unlike the other passageways, this one was perfectly straight and so long its walls seemed to meet in the distance. Given how different it was, Thris suspected any blockage would be different too. He did not know whether that meant they were to escape the stone or die amongst it.

He wondered whether angels had ended their lives here before and whether the wraiths were angel essence, confined and perverted. To be denied the Great Beyond, even in death, was too terrible even to contemplate.

'I do not like this,' murmured Ky.

'Neither do I,' admitted Thris. The sameness of the stone was mesmerising, and he half imagined he was in a rift that would deliver him to a new fold, and when the passage finally terminated, he almost believed it had.

'I do not understand,' whispered Ky.

They were in a broad circular room, walled in the same black stone as the passages, with a circular pool at its centre. An even band of lush foliage occupied the space between the wall and the water's edge, and waterlilies floated on the water's surface, their blue-tipped blooms heavily perfumed. 'There is a rift here,' said Thris slowly, his gaze on the flowers.

'I do not sense it,' said Ky in confusion.

'It is under the water.'

'But . . . surely it is more likely to be among the plant caste? I know your rift sensitivity is greater than mine but even you are fallible, as you have admitted.'

Ky smiled to soften his words but Thris's thoughts were on the water rift in the Dendrinai. He knew of no angel who had transited it, the risk of drowning too great. 'We will search the plant caste,' he said, and Ky nodded eagerly. They set off in opposite directions and were soon back at their starting point.

'Nothing,' said Ky and eyed the pool uneasily. 'Are you sure the resonance comes from the water?'

'Yes, but I will confirm it,' said Thris, and stepped gingerly into the pool. The water was warm, and the bottom covered in a soft mud that oozed between his toes. He felt his way forward, sending circular ripples to shore and causing the waterlilies to swirl about him in a moving circle of blue.

The bottom suddenly disappeared and he swam gently, the rift's hum growing as he neared the pool's centre, then he trod water and looked down. The water was too dark to see anything, even his body had disappeared, as if he had already been claimed.

He shivered but Ky watched him anxiously and he kept his expression calm. 'I am going to take a quick look under the water,' he called back to him, and let himself sink. It was completely different to the underwater world of Crystal Lake. Here his corporeal form was so shadowy he touched his chest to reassure himself he was still there.

He surfaced and swam on to the centre of the pool. The hum told him he was directly above the rift and he dived. The waterlilies' stems came from all around him to form a single twisted rope that disappeared palely into the rift's dark heart. The stems might serve as a guide in their transit, or end, *or* he and Ky might simply run out of breath. He swam back to shore and described what he had seen. 'I sense it is our only way out,' he finished.

48

'Rifts might have opened in the other passages by now,' said Ky.

'It is possible they are opening and closing all around us,' confirmed Thris, 'but the passage that led us here was different, and *here* is different too. I think we are *meant* to take this rift, Ky.'

'You think the Principae direct us?'

'I do not know but like the Great Beyond, the Principae allow us free will. We *chose* to leave Ezam and, in making that choice, possibilities opened to us that we were denied in Ezam.'

'Like death,' said Ky grimly.

'Yes, but also a deeper understanding. The speed and strength that served me in Ezam failed me once I left. I attacked the shekinah, Ky, and injured her again when I *chose* to obey my mentor's instructions to seduce her.'

'The shekinah *made* you—' began Ky indignantly.

'They were *my* choices, Ky, and they forced me to consider what I am. I am less than I was before the Guideship, but perhaps I am also more.'

'If only we knew whether these choices aided ascension,' cried Ky in frustration. 'Are there no scrolls in the Bokos that speak of such things?'

'I do not know, but Prime-archae Serith might. We can ask him on our return.'

'*If* we return.'

There was a short silence. 'How long can you hold your breath?' asked Thris. Ky shrugged and Thris smiled grimly. 'I have never tested myself either. Let us conduct a little experiment to see what is possible.'

They settled by the pool's edge and took turns in counting how long the other could hold their breath and decided that, if they had not exited the rift by the count of forty-five, they must turn back.

They swam to where the rift's vibrations were strongest but as Thris prepared to dive, Ky caught his arm. 'I can't do this, Thris.' He swallowed convulsively. 'I'm not strong like you. I fear so many things.'

Thris faced him as they trod water. 'I fear many things too,' he said. 'I fear I will fail the shekinah, that I will fail you, *and* that I will fail Ash. He's trapped in the White Helixai, Ky, and I need your help to set him free.' Thris softened his voice. 'All you need to do is swim and count. It's been *your* counting that's kept us safe. Will you count with me one last time, Ky? For Ash?'

Ky's eyes were wide with fear but he nodded, and they embraced. 'Forty-five,' said Thris, took a deep breath, and dived.

The darkness blinded him, and he went hand over hand down the rope of twisted stems, deeper and deeper, counting steadily. He glanced back once to confirm Ky followed but the darkness was empty, and he could not afford to check a second time. The water remained warm, which helped, but the blackness pressed in on him like a physical force.

Thirty went by, then thirty-five. The blackness endured. Forty, forty-one, forty-two. Thris strained ahead. Forty-three, forty-four, forty-five. Time to turn back. He swung around and light flared, but it was not Ezam's gentle peach or the light of an alien fold; it was the spectres.

They swarmed between him and the way back and he had no choice but to haul himself deeper into the darkness. It was pointless counting. Thoughts of Ky and of the horrible death that awaited them tumbled through his brain, but mostly he thought of sweet, sweet air.

He shut his eyes as his strength failed and then something cannoned into him and knocked the last of the precious breath from his lungs. His mouth jerked open reflexively, but there was no rush of water down his throat. He was on dry land.

He lay facedown, sucking in air and there was a thump as Ky landed beside him and guzzled air just as voraciously. 'I do not care where we are,' muttered Ky, 'as long as it is dry.'

Thris rolled onto his back and gazed up at the umber sky. 'We are home,' he said hoarsely.

'Indeed, you are,' said a voice.

Prime-archae Serith observed them from the glis and Thris struggled upright to bow and palm. Ky only made it to his knees but Serith did not seem to notice. 'Two of the three,' he murmured. 'The third is confined by light. Have you come back to release him?'

'Yes,' said Thris, taken aback. '*If* I can.'

'The blue angel Senquar-archae spoke of such things,' continued Serith dreamily. '*Light is the lure and light the trap; light the maze and light the map. The red, the blue, and the white won't show, what mantise, scarab and sumi know.*' He smiled beatifically but Thris found the mention of a maze ominous.

'And what of you?' asked Serith, turning to Ky. 'What have you come back for?'

'To learn from you at the Bokos.'

Thris's head swivelled in surprise. Ky's chest heaved as his body restored itself, but his face was calm. It was as if the old Ky had returned but there was an openness about him now that had been absent before.

51

Joy for his friend surged, but sadness too because Thris knew their paths had finally diverged. Serith moved off and Ky enclosed Thris in an intense hug. 'You know where to find me,' he said. 'You are going to the White Helixai?'

'To Archae Kald first. A visit that is long overdue.'

'He will be angered by what has happened.'

'And rightly so.'

'You have done nothing wrong,' said Ky urgently. 'You have . . .' He glanced anxiously in the direction Serith had gone.

'Go,' said Thris. 'I will come to the Bokos later. To retrieve Ash, I will need Prime-archae Serith's advice and that of Ash's friend, Prime-archae Mirek.' Ky nodded and sped off through the glis.

Chapter 9

Thris had met with Archae Kald many times since becoming his protégé, but he only thought of their first meeting as he made his way through the Halls. He had won an entire round of trials and had been exhausted and elated when the summons had come.

The interview had been brief, but the Archae had bestowed on him the blessings of a mentorship that would hasten Thris's ascension *and* the Archae's transcendence. Thris had been determined never to fail his mentor's trust, and he had not, until the Guideship.

He knocked on the Archae's door, was given permission to enter, bowed and palmed. The Archae reclined on a couch by the window and his gaze remained on the scene below for a considerable time. Thris waited and the Archae eventually roused, poured himself a goblet of ambrosia, and held it to the light as if he examined its purity.

'I expected your presence long before this,' he said finally, his cold gaze on Thris. 'I have conversed with your Shadow yet you have not deigned to visit. Nor have you obeyed my explicit instructions to return my daughter here.'

Thris bowed again. 'I beg your pardon, Archae. We were attacked before I could do so. Ky was injured and I became separated from you daughter. I returned Ky to Ezam with the intention of immediately returning to retrieve your daughter, but Ky's wounds remained unhealed and, when he transited again, I followed to protect him. We became confined in a strange fold and have only just returned. I know where your daughter is and, with your permission, will retrieve her.'

'You do not appear to *need* my permission for your actions, Dane,' he said, coming to his feet. 'My instructions were clear. The Shadow was irrelevant to them.'

'He was injured. I could not abandon—'

'So, you abandoned *my* directives and *my* daughter instead!'

'It was not my intention—'

'Do not dare to argue with an Archae, *Dane*!' roared Kald. Thris dropped his head and the Archae circled him, leaving a fume in his wake as bitter as Moth Fold's. 'I see you have joined with the shekinah,' he said. 'At least you executed *that* part of my instructions. Did you find it enjoyable?'

'No,' said Thris, recalling with shame his actions in the cave.

Kald laughed. 'Oh, it can be, I assure you,' he said. 'And make no mistake, Dane, you have given the shekinah a taste for more and you will use that *appetite* to return her here.'

'I do not think it will be enough, Archae,' murmured Thris, his gaze still on the floor.

'Oh, it will be, especially if you *feed* it.' There was silence and Thris heard the chink of crystal as Kald replenished his drink. 'You have seen her wings?' he asked.

'Yes, Archae.'

'What does that tell you?'

'I do not know what to think, Archae.'

'I have clearly fathered her more than once, Dane. She carries my blood doubly. Once you retrieve her, she will be passed to the Principae. A daimon with Iahhel traits cannot be left to roam the rifts.'

Thris raised his eyes in shock. *Viv was not to be reunited with her mother*! He expected to see sorrow in the Archae's face but, if anything, he looked smug.

'You will leave immediately and return her immediately,' said the Archae. 'Is that understood, Dane?'

'Yes, Archae.'

Archae Kald turned his back and Thris realised he had been dismissed. He bowed and palmed, then exited the room and pulled the door softly shut behind him. He no longer had a mentor, but Dane were still obliged to obey their superiors.

He took to the air, his thoughts on Ash as he alighted at Haven to retrieve clothes and a pack, then took to the air again and came to ground at the rift that led to Hearth Fold. Ash remained confined by the White Helixai and the Archae's orders gave Thris no choice but to leave him there. At least Ky was free from risk now and Prime-archae Serith's wisdom might free Ash in Thris's absence.

The rift was open, but he hesitated. The glis chimed softly around him, bronzed by the umber sky, and love for his home and friends surged anew 'Stay safe,' he murmured, and stepped into the rift.

Viv had little memory of how the night passed. The rapist's injuries went beyond the physical, as did those the arsehole had added, and had she a knife, she would have used it on herself not the leash, to escape once and for all.

The Pool Zadic came and went, an oily glow behind the heavy clouds, and Viv sloughed citrus as the leash hauled her along. And then it rained, drops that pelted as hard as gravel. The urrut bowed their faces before it but Viv raised her face and let it pound her, and in some strange way, it washed her clean.

The storm did not last long and then the sky lightened, and the new sun warmed her skin. The wet urrut smelled richly of animal and huffed their hot breath over her, thick with the scent of chewed grass. They plodded along like ships that rocked in a swell, and she became aware of their soft whiffles and grunts.

They sounds rippled up and down the group as if the urrut at the back assured those at the front they followed. But followed *where*? To the hated *cloud-crawlers who had seeded her*, according to the arsehole. Viv recalled the winged figure on Poss's mirror. *If* there were angels in this fold, and *if* her mother had transited here, she might still be here, though not in Vales where her looks would attract the same hatred as Viv's.

But even *if* her mother were in the Astraali city, Viv might never reach her. *She won't survive the journey*, Sehereden had said. Viv's jaw clenched and she fingered the lock under her chin. It felt ornate but she could not see it and turned her attention to the lock that connected her to tether rope. Even after years of thieving, Viv had never seen anything like it.

It was the length of her index finger and composed of strands of wire woven together. There was a join in the middle and lacy holes that could be keyholes or decoration. She pressed gently along the lock's length and listened as she turned the ends in opposite directions and in the same direction. Nothing happened. One of the holes might be a keyhole but she had not seen the arsehole use a key, not that she had been looking.

The lock would have to be simple given how often the Stonash must tether and untether the urrut but then she saw the urrut's leashes were simply knotted to the tether rope. It seemed the arsehole had procured a lock just for her.

Keyed locks were pickable, *if* you had a piece of wire, or a ring-pull, or a hairclip and if the lock were not keyed, the clicking sound might be a screw-type mechanism coming into alignment.

Viv gently pushed, probed and pressured the metal, all to no avail. At least she had time on her side, she concluded sourly. The peak that housed the Astraali city would be many days away at the speed they travelled.

The urrut might be slow but they went without pause and the caravan left the val behind, mounted the ridge-side and ascended along its shoulder to reach the crest around midday. Then it turned north, *the same direction the rapist had gone*. Viv's heart gave a sickening thud. He might lurk nearby, and she was right at the back of the caravan and easy to snatch!

The rats of memory barred their teeth and Viv struggled to think of Thris, of the need to survive to see him again, and of her mother, but it was no use. She stumbled into the urrut, barely able to keep her feet, but they did not seem to mind, and after a time their earthy animal smell calmed her enough to think again.

The ridge top was wide enough for the urrut to go side by side and dung and the hanks of fleece caught on bushes told her it was a well-used route but there was no water and Viv's thirst grew. Maybe the urrut were like camels that carried water in their fat and maybe they had to because there was no water *at all* on the journey.

Was that why Sehereden said she would not survive? Normally a lack of water would not have bothered her but injury always triggered thirst and she dredged through what she knew of the elddra. The man in the cave said they did not need to pee, which was true of her, and the arsehole had made some comment about them being different too. *The elddra do not suffer as we do.* She had thought it sarcasm, for she certainly did feel pain, but maybe daimon *were* different here, in fact, daimon might be different in *every* fold.

As the day drew on, her need to drink even overtook her need to undo the lock. She hoped to God when they stopped for the night it would be near a soak or spring, but when she heard the horn ring out to bring the urrut to a halt, there was no water in sight.

Chapter 10

The urrut lowered their front halves to the ground and their massive rumps followed with a thump as they settled for the night, and soon only Viv remained standing. The urruts' mustard-coloured backs stretched away before her and while she could see no Stonash, she soon smelled their cooking fires.

Viv's hopes rose as a Stonash appeared around the side of the beasts. He seemed to be checking whether everything was in order, but his gaze moved over her as if she were not there. 'I need water,' she said quickly but he completed his inspection and headed back towards the head of the caravan. 'Water!' she screamed after him, but she knew he was not coming back.

She jerked at the collar in fury and wondered exactly what sort of deal the arsehole had made. Perhaps it was to drag her along till she died and then drag her corpse, in fact, they might not be going to the Astraali city at all.

The odour of cooked food drifted back, and Viv licked her parched lips. No doubt the arsehole ate too *and* drank in the company of his *loyal* lein but where was *her* lein? Taken by the arsehole and his friends? Taken by the Waradi? Lost and alone in the darkness? She was enveloped in a tart vapour and struggled to calm. She *had* to believe Poss was smart enough to complete the last part of the journey on her own or there was no point in going on.

The wind freshened and she crouched beside an urrut, using its bulk as shelter. It was cold on the ridge top and she wondered how much colder it would get before she reached the snow-capped peak, *if* she reached the snow-capped peak. The urrut rested peacefully and she stroked it tentatively, but it got to its feet and Viv rose too, sorry to have disturbed it and wary of being trodden on.

The wind had gained an icy edge but all she felt was relief because it carried the unmistakable scent of rain. The urrut she had disturbed moved restlessly and Viv strained into the darkness her thoughts on the Waradi rapist and other predators. His men had fled well before he did, and she was the reason. *I own you, lein-tryst, remember that.* The bastard did *not* own her, *no one* owned her, and no one *ever* would!

The rain was freezing but she welcomed it and used her elbow to channel it to her mouth, slurping it down until she was sated. The rain ended as quickly as it began, leaving her cold and wet. The urrut she had disturbed was unhappy too, grunting and throwing its head back towards its tail and Viv realised in shock it was about to birth.

She strained away as far as the leash allowed as she recalled tales of farmers being chased across paddocks by previously docile cows. The urrut lay down again and beat its great head against the ground, and Viv debated whether to shout for the Stonash but doubted they would come anyway.

She had seen plenty of nature shows that said animals birthed easily, unlike humans, but no one knew how much pain animals really suffered, and she watched it anxiously. The urrut seemed to be gentle beasts and she wanted this one, and its calf, to survive.

The wind filled with Poss's asht-voices and then, as the clouds glowed with the zadic's light, there was a sloshing sound and the calf slithered onto the ground. It was still enclosed in its birth sack and while the urrut clambered to its feet and licked it clean, the calf remained motionless. 'Please God,' whispered Viv. The cloud shredded and the zadic showed the little body. *Please God, please God, please God* and then the calf gave a soft mewl. 'Thank you,' she muttered and sleeved her eyes.

It managed to stand and disappeared under the curtain of fleece to feed and Viv's heart lurched as the urrut settled on the ground, but then the calf reappeared and nestled at its side. The zadic lit them, mother and child, and in some odd way, Viv was reminded of how Lettie had held her in the dark while Jimmy Wright had raged.

Viv was no longer that child and nor, she realised abruptly, was her mother that woman. Viv knew her life on the streets had changed her, but she had not considered how her mother might have changed too. Lettie might have remarried, had another family, and not want to be reminded of her old life. Then again, after Jimmy Wright, she might have sworn off men and yearn for the child she left behind.

What ya think, Vivi? Wanna flip a coin? Rim's voice intruded. No, arsehole, I do not want to flip a coin. If Lettie's experiences were like Viv's, she might have sworn off angels too, although the jury was still out on Thris. Viv chewed her lip. There were lots of black marks against the beautiful Thris, including doing her father's bidding, being loyal to Ky, and attacking her while damaged by Moth Fold. *Ya excusing a would-be rapist now, eh Vivi*?

Rim's scathing accusation was right but nothing Thris had done or failed to do now made any difference. They had been bound from the moment his wings had folded over hers and turned the world to stars.

The zadic faded but when the new day dawned and the urrut rose, the calf stayed on the ground. It had only suckled once and when the Stonash did his usual rounds she yelled at him and pointed to the calf. His blank eyes

61

passed over it as they passed over her and he disappeared back around the side.

The horn sounded and the calf's mother bellowed as the collar pulled her forward. Viv willed the calf to follow and then, as the slack in her own leash disappeared, managed to get a hand on the calf's back leg. The collar choked her, but she hung on, having to drag the calf along the ground before she could haul it into her arms.

It was heavy and Viv shrugged out of her jacket and, with a great deal of swearing, got the calf into the same jacket-sling she had used for Poss. She probably carried the calf to its death, for the urrut might be traded for meat, but she refused to abandon it.

Chapter 11

Thris exited the rift into Hearth Fold, sought out the trees where he had sheltered with Viv, and secreted himself in the branches to wait for the fold's dark cycle. He could pass through Hearth Fold without thanking the Keeper, as he had last time, but then he had been injured and now he was healed.

Waiting gave him ample time to consider his former mentor's claim of having fathered Viv more than once. The time differences between folds made it possible but it was odd the Archae had sensed no angel essence in Viv's mother. It also contradicted the Tome's assertion that daimon were sterile.

Archae Kald believed Viv's parentage gave reason for her wings but the Rynth's uncountable possibilities meant that while nine-hundred and ninety-nine daimon might be wingless, the thousandth could be winged. Similarly, nine-hundred and ninety-nine daimon could be insensitive to rifts, and the thousandth sense them. But if the thousandth *winged-daimon* were also rift aware?

The rarity of such a phenomenon supported Archae Kald's claim but did not *prove* it and his heart quickened as he saw the same argument applied to him. Sexual congress might inhibit the ascension of nine-hundred and ninety-nine Dane, but not the thousandth and the proof of that was in Archaes Kald and Dejon's ascension.

Then again, their ascension might be due to their *exemplary* actions outweighing their sexual transgressions, and not only did he lack *exemplary* actions, he was increasingly unclear what made actions *exemplary.* Obeying Archae Kald's instruction to join with Viv should have been exemplary but he sensed it was not, while their second *angelic* joining, which should have damned him, had healed him instead.

His second joining had lacked the deceit of the first, he perceived, and now Archae Kald ordered him to repeat his initial deceit to retrieve Viv and send her to Crystal Fold, not to her mother's fold as the Archae and *he* had pledged. Thris was bound to obey an Archae but he had no idea what the Principae intended and for the first in countless cycles, he must decide what to do without a mentor's aid.

Thris quit the trees as soon as it was dark and made his way to the Keeper's Haven. It took a long time for his knock to be answered and at first, he thought it was another Keeper. She was bent and her face heavily lined, but her green eyes were the same.

He followed her in and settled at the table while she rummaged in a cupboard and finally produced a stoppered jug and two glasses. They rattled as she set them down and then sat opposite. 'I remember you,' she whispered in a gravelly voice, 'even though most of my life has passed since last you were here.' She paused while she concentrated on filling the glasses. 'You kept company with a daimon. I've thought since how hard it must be to be half as you are, beautiful and unageing, and half as I am. Is she still with you?'

'She is in another fold.'

'Is she happy there?' Thris hesitated and the Keeper dipped her head. 'Forgive my impertinence. It's just *my* human heart worrying about *her* human heart.' The woman leaned forward. 'My daughter sleeps now, for she's lately birthed a little one, Keepers both. I don't think I will see your kind again.'

Thris had no antidote for human caste death and simply raised his glass. 'The Host of Ezam thanks the Keeper for guarding the way,' he said and emptied it.

'The Keeper thanks the Host for the blessings of angels,' she responded. 'And wishes the daimon both human and angelic happiness,' she added with a smile.

The rift out of Hearth Fold was close to the trees and exited to Moth Fold, as Thris knew it would. It was his third trek to the putrid mountains and the cave where he had attacked Viv, and he harmonised before he entered. Ky had carried him last time, but now he was strong enough to endure its corrosion alone and he arrived in Sand Fold intact.

He harmonised again and set off quickly up the first of the hills, noticing for the first time how the gold contrasted with the green of Hearth Fold, the green vines and mantises of the Dendrinai, and the Thorny Mountain's Green Helixai.

Green was associated with death in many folds which was why the Green Helixai had never attracted him. Green things withered and died, as the green-eyed Keeper had reminded him, but Ezam was not immune from decay either, it simply happened more slowly.

He sensed the subtle vibrations of a rift but hesitated, knowing it exited into the fold where he had been torn apart. The Principae had put him back together but it had been Viv who had *restored* him, not to his previous self, but to something better and armed with this comforting understanding, he stepped into the rift.

Beast Fold was in its dark cycle and the sky ablaze with its brilliant red, yellow, and green stars while its jungle was filled with the howls of beastmen. Thris took to the air in search of a safe place to wait out the dark and landed on the ledge of a cave on one of the peaks.

He confirmed the cave was empty but kept his wings unbedded as the beastmen's cries drifted up from below. Beastmen looked like a cross between human and animal castes, but appearances could be deceptive, as daimon caste had proved. Angel and human castes might look similar, but they were fundamentally different and for the first time Thris pondered how daimon caste functioned *emotionally*.

He had considered how Viv's emotions impeded her ability to harmonise, sense for rifts, and stay safe, but he had not sought to safeguard her well-being for her own sake and neither had Archae Kald. Green starlight threw his shadow against the stone and he recalled the green-eyed Keeper's questions about Viv's happiness. The Keeper's questions were as insolent as his own doubts about Archae Kald's motives, but they reminded him Viv was half *human* and that was important.

He took to the air as soon as it was light to search for the rift Viv had used to exit. He went to the cavern she had occupied first and hovered a safe distance from its lip. The beastman was absent but its young were ensconced in a nest of leaves, their human-like legs entwined, and their cat-like tails curled about them in sleep.

The mother would not be far away and Thris flew in the direction he had seen Ky and the beastman take on his first visit but could find no break in the canopy. It had probably grown over which meant he must search for the rift from the ground. He landed but his skin crawled as he moved through the tangle. It was an unpleasant manifestation of fear, an emotion common in folds like Moonsun, and one that fed hatred. He had sensed both in Viv early in her time in Ezam.

The Tome did not describe how daimon reconciled their human emotions with their angelic ones and Thris paused. He had thought the conundrums he faced were the conflicts between his Guideship, Archae Kald's new orders, and Viv's wishes, but now he saw the reconciliation of angelic and human traits was part of them too.

Chapter 12

Thris reached the pool where he had swum and stopped in shock as he sensed Viv's resonance, dismayed he had missed it earlier. Then he recalled his swim had been interrupted by Ash's urgent summons to aid Ky.

The rift to Sand Fold had closed and he searched the surrounding area. The Tome devoted countless pages to the predictability or otherwise of rifts without reaching firm conclusions and visiting members of human caste had variously called their openings and closings luck, magic, and coincidence.

Whatever the truth, Thris had so far enjoyed a lot of luck, magic or coincidence, but as he searched in vain for a rift and green stars blinked into being once more, he became aware of a resonance potent with human caste intelligence and big cat cunning, and it was *very* close. 'Ash,' he whispered urgently. 'I need your help.'

Ash's long meditation in the White Helixai came to an abrupt end as a shaft of green light impaled him like a spear. He flung up his hand but the vision of Thris poured into him like a draught of ambrosia that like ambrosia, warmed and restored him.

The pristine beauty of the White Helixai brittled to a frigid emptiness and Ash struggled from the slab, staggered back through the shining caverns, and collapsed onto the ledge outside. The stone's coarseness was akin to violence against his skin and Ezam's garish sky assaulted his senses like blows. A part of him yearned to return to the White Helixai's ethereal emptiness where his spirit resonated with the purity of chimes, but a larger part craved a world made manifest.

Opening a rift for Thris to exit Beastman Fold was many times simpler than escaping the White Helixai's allure and it seemed an age before Ezam's sky gentled to something less abrasive. He felt as though he had journeyed far and yet remained where he was, as if he had learned everything and knew nothing. He brought his wings over himself for comfort and was unsurprised to see only the tips remained blue.

White could mean the *absence* of colour not the *presence* of wisdom, but the old belief no longer fitted, and he winged away towards the Bokos, taking in the softness of the Thorny Mountains' grey and Glass Lake's gleaming aqua. The colours thrilled him as if he were new to Ezam and saw them for the first time.

He came to ground near the Bokos but did not go in. The lush brightness of nearby vines held him, and he was still transfixed by them when Prime-archae Serith found him. Ash did not notice the Prime-archae for some time and then his gaze fastened on the Prime-archae's green robe and he forgot to bow and palm.

'Tell me of your time in the White Helixai,' said the Prime-archae, giving no sign he had noticed the omission.

Ash managed to describe the ethereal light and purity of the stone but struggled to remember what he had thought, felt, and done during his long absence. He fell silent and his gaze drifted back to the vines.

'Three angels,' said Prime-archae Serith softly. 'Three angels but no longer together. Did Thrisdane release you?'

Ash blinked. 'No . . . yes. He was in need and there was green . . .' he trailed off aware he made no sense.

69

The Prime-archae nodded sagely. *'Light is the lure and light the trap; light the maze and light the map. The red, the blue, and the white won't show, what mantise, scarab and sumi know.* The words of another blue angel, Ashdane. Do they aid you?'

'I do not know,' said Ash, struggling to focus.

'Not knowing is a start, but where will it end?' There was a long pause. 'Kydane is within,' he murmured as he moved away and was soon lost among the glis.

Ash dragged himself away from the green, keen to see Ky and puzzled why he no longer Shadowed Thris. He found Ky by a window surrounded by scrolls that scattered as Ky leapt up and embraced him. 'You have been away too long,' said Ky thickly.

'We both have,' said Ash and settled at the table.

'I am no longer Shadow,' said Ky as he gathered the scrolls. 'I lacked the strength to withstand the horrors of the Rynth.' He gave a shaky smile. 'Prime-archae Serith says accepting your weaknesses is a sign of strength. I do not know but being with Thris put him in even more danger, so perhaps it is best I am here.'

'But why *here*?' asked Ash, glancing at the gloomy recesses.

'Why the *White Helixai*?' returned Ky with a smile, then sobered. 'Thris and I ended up in a maze and were forced to escape through a water rift. I controlled my fear by counting and I realised I wanted to know more about how things could be controlled.'

'And Archae Dejon?'

'I have not controlled my fear that much,' confessed Ky. 'Thris visited Archae Kald on our return and I have not seen him since. I think the Archae ordered Thris back

70

into the rifts. The Archae wants the shekinah returned to Ezam.'

'Thris was in Beast Fold but he is not there now.'

'Beast Fold?' said Ky in surprise. 'Was the shekinah with him?'

'I did not sense her.'

'Prime-archae Mirek said you were confined by the White Helixai. He was greatly concerned.'

'I *was* at the White Helixai, but I was not confined. I was . . .' The Helixai's purity seemed dream-like now but as his thoughts returned there, it was the Bokos that faded, and Ky who was stripped of substance. The obliteration of the manifest by the ethereal jolted Ash and his wings fluttered.

'Your wings are all but white,' gasped Ky. 'What happened there, Ash? What did you endure at the White Helixai?'

'I endured nothing! My wings are white, but I remain undeserving! I am *unnatural*!'

Ky leaned across the table. 'Prime-archae Serith speaks of another blue angel,' he said urgently. 'This has happened before.'

'But for what purpose?' cried Ash, pacing the small space. 'I should have stayed in the White Helixai where I could do no harm.'

'And what harm could you possibly do here?' asked Prime-archae Mirek, appearing from around the shelves.

Ash bowed and palmed but the Prime-archae grasped his shoulders so Ash must look at him. 'White plumage is *never* a sign of evil, Ashdane.' Ash took a shuddering breath and Mirek guided him to the chair, poured ambrosia, and insisted he drink.

'I cannot claim to know how the Blue Helixai affected you,' said Mirek. 'Your time there was before our friendship, but your ordeal in the Red Helixai, where you fled its flames, and your long sojourn in the White, gifted you signs of transcendence. The blue angel Senquar-archae spent time at the White and wrote of it but his words are riddling. Kydane and I have sought to decipher them without success.'

'Prime-archae Serith spoke of them,' said Ash in small voice. 'They make no sense to me either.'

'Not even after the cycles you spent in the White?' asked Mirek. Ash shook his head. 'I feared I had lost you,' said Mirek softly. 'The scrolls say Senquar-archae disappeared and while it is *thought* he transcended little is known.'

The exploits of the other blue angel disturbed Ash, and he took a gulp of ambrosia. Senquar-archae's experiences suggested a precedent for Ash's marks of ascension, but no one knew how Senquar-archae's time in Ezam had ended or *the damage he had done*. Senquar-archae might have been erased from Ezam's records for very good reasons.

'I have the chance to discover more of Senquar-archae,' said Ky eagerly, 'for I search where no other angel searches. The Bokos is vast but no matter where I wander, I always find my way back. Sometimes my steps number in the thousands.'

Ash nodded but even if Ky found the relevant scroll, its contents might end hope rather than gift it. The belief he was unnatural grew and he glanced about nervously.

'What thoughts occupied you in the White Helixai?' asked Mirek, as he topped up Ash's goblet.

'I have no memory of them, or of my time there. It is as if I returned to the place before Ezam.'

'It was starry?'

Ash shook his head. 'It was empty and yet I felt no lack until Thris summoned me.'

'Thrisdane summoned you?' said Mirek sharply.

'He was in Beast Fold . . . at least I assume it was Beast Fold. There was so much green . . .'

'Ah,' said Mirek. 'I believe we have our answer, Kydane.' Ky and Ash looked at the Prime-archae in mystification, and Mirek smiled. *Light is the lure and light the trap; light the maze and light the map. The red, the blue, and the white won't show, what mantise, scarab and sumi know.* Senquar-archae surely refers to the Helixai, and in the first part, specifically to the White Helixai. The only Helixai he does not mention by name is the Green, which you have yet to visit, Ashdane.'

'I think I understand,' said Ky excitedly. 'The White Helixai attracted you, Ash. It *lured* you, but you were stuck there, though you did not know it, but somehow it told you something useful too, that is the bit about the map. A map is something that human caste use to find their way about,' he added.

'I believe Kydane is correct,' said Mirek, 'and that the last part of Senquar-archae's words suggest that while the Red, Blue and White Helixai are each useful in their own ways to your transcendence, so too is the Green.'

'The Green?' repeated Ash fearfully.

'It is *what mantise, scarab and sumi know*,' said Mirek gently. 'All three live their lives among Ezam's green.' No one said anything and Ash wrapped his wings about himself for comfort. 'I have work to do,' said Mirek, suddenly business-like, 'as does Kydane. But spend some time together first, as friends should who have been parted.

73

You know where I am, Ashdane, if you desire further speech.'

Mirek's footsteps receded, and it was Ky who broke the silence. 'You do not *have* to go to the Green Helixai, Ash.'

'We both know I do.'

'Well, you do not have to go immediately,' he amended. 'Stay in the Bokos with me. There is so much here we could explore together and the Prime-archaes are kind. Not like . . .' he trailed off.

'You will need to visit your mentor one last time,' said Ash gently.

'Yes, but not yet.' He paused. 'I feel I have come home, Ash, and it is so strange that I never knew it before.'

'I am glad for you, Ky. Tell me of your travels with Thris in my absence.'

'It is a long tale.'

'I am in no rush,' said Ash bleakly, and dredged up a smile.

Chapter 13

Viv trudged along carrying the calf, her head filled with endless questions about Thris. Had he sensed her resonance when he rescued Ky from the pig-bear? And if so, was he on his way back? And if not but Ky was now safe in Ezam, had he resumed his search for her? And if so, where was he now?

She considered Ky's claim Ash had spoken into his head and that Archae Kald had ordered Thris to return Viv to Ezam. Thris had sworn to take her to her mother and even if her *beloved* father had changed his mind, she was holding Thris to his pledge.

Thoughts of him woke an unbearable longing. She craved his nearness and scent; his wings around her; and the bond that went beyond sex and stars and stopped her from being utterly alone.

She hugged the calf close for comfort and when they stopped that night, she helped it suckle. It seemed sturdier afterwards, its chin beaded with milk, its little belly bulging. The calf suckled later that night too and the next morning, and when they set off again, Viv let it walk, although she kept a careful eye on it. It was already bigger, its fleece in silken ringlets, its horns nubs on the top of its head. Viv called it *calf*, when she called it anything at all, and was determined not to grow attached to it.

The caravan continued along the ridge tops, the path descending and ascending as one ridge gave way to the next, but always going up. The land fell away to either side and Viv might have enjoyed the sweeping vistas had she not been hauled along on a leash.

They were in their sixth day of travel when she heard a high-pitched keening. There was no wind and she stared about uneasily. The urrut showed no signs of alarm, even when the light dwindled to an odd sort of twilight, but then, without warning, the temperature plummeted. The cold was so ferocious Viv's breath was scoured from her throat, and then she was hit by the driest, coldest wind she had ever known.

The urrut lumbered on, heads down, but only the leash kept Viv moving. The wind burned like fire and, as Sehereden's warning echoed in her head, she clawed her way up the tether rope and in amongst the urrut. Being half angel was not going to save her, she realised in panic, the skin on her hands already cracked and her lips blistered. She was thirsty too and that only happened in extremity.

The Stonash's flattened faces and thickened skin were explicable now, as were the urruts' heavy fleece, which *she could use too*. Viv stumbled to the side of the nearest beast and forced her wooden hands into action. She knotted hanks of fleece into loops, then hooked her arms through one set and swung herself forward to get her feet through the others. Once attached, she crossed her arms across her chest to lock herself in place and wriggled until she was hard up against the urrut's rumbling belly, so its fleece fell over her like a blanket.

The fleece blunted the worst of the cold, but its brutality exhausted her, and she fell into a doze, not waking until the urrut came to a stop. Twilight still held the land and the wind wailed, but the urrut settled on the ground as if it were a normal night.

The calf suckled, and Viv crept out and suckled too. The milk was warm and sweet, and she drank as greedily as the calf, then clambered back into her sanctuary. They went on again the next morning, but the horrendous cold was unrelenting, and the days slipped into a nightmarish routine. Viv dozed during the day, hooked under the urrut's fleece, and suckled with the calf when they stopped.

Her face hardened and her lips bled but the fleece provided warmth, dozing conserved strength, and the milk gave her just enough sustenance to survive. The world became a horror movie of shrieking wind and murky light, and Viv's awareness shrank until all that remained was a desperate need to hang on.

Ataghan and Sehereden set camp less than a day's ride from Esh-accom. They could have ridden on, but Ataghan was in no hurry to reach the settlement. Esh-accom was too crowded for his liking, with its noise and close-packed houses, and the excruciating sound of children's laughter in its streets.

The Sylds awaited his return but Ataghan knew only blades defeated blades, not words. The Cascade Zadic ignited the sky and he stared at it sightlessly. Horse Zadic had held the heavens at the fighting's start, but he had no idea which zadic would rule when the fighting ended. What he did know was that there would be no peace until his knives had claimed those whose hate had destroyed Esh-embrin. Heat seared him at how close he had come to their leader and their fruitless search since. The Vorash's stinking weather had not helped but there would be no failure next time!

Sehereden's *yu* intruded, its music tinged with longing rather than sadness, and the burn of Ataghan's body eased. Sehereden knew when to speak and when to stay silent, and the firelight showed a face honed by fighting and journeying, but also that of the true and open boy Ataghan had sworn leinship with.

Chance had given them a physical similarity that strangers mistook for brotherhood but looks were irrelevant. Leinships were of the heart, not of the skin. The Eshadi believed them a sign of Enda's benevolence, given their resemblance to lein-trysts, but Ataghan did not share the Eshadi's belief in Enda's goodwill *or* in Soaich's ill will, for that matter. The present fighting had nothing to do with gods.

The music ended and Sehereden packed the yu away. 'How long will you stay in Esh-accom?' he asked.

'Enough time for Taris to rest.'

'And then?'

'I resume the hunt.'

'You should rest for a time too,' said Sehereden. 'You've spent fewer than two days in a single place since this began.'

'And I won't until it ends.'

'There's likely to be a lull soon, if not an ending,' said Sehereden, his gaze on the sky. 'It's hard to imagine Waradi or Ascadi risking their chances to father.'

'Most of what's happened was hard to imagine before Horse Zadic,' grated Ataghan. Sehereden made no reply but his restlessness was clear. Cascade Zadic's rippling flow marked the slow build to Fire Zadic, with its festivities, tournaments, and couplings, and if men were fortunate, come Glimwing, there would be choose- or seed-children gifted, and perhaps even lein-trysts.

78

'I don't ask that you hunt with me,' said Ataghan. 'You need time away from the fighting.'

Sehereden's eyes flashed in the firelight. 'We *both* need time away. The smaller setts will come into Esh-accom soon anyway for the trial tournaments and the women consider their choices. We can set patrols, or we can go out again if necessary. We need time to eat in peace, At, and sleep in beds, and speak of things other than war. We need time to enjoy the company of women.'

'You want me to *replace* Fariye, lein? Is that what you're saying?'

'Nothing can replace Fariye *or* the other lost children,' said Sehereden gently. 'But you must let yourself heal.'

'I'll heal when I've sent every last one of Esh-embrin's murderers into the fires without their amés; when I *know* they'll spend eternity wandering lost in death; when no Waradi or Ascadi will *ever* turn their knives our way again!'

'But I wonder whether it will be too late by then,' said Sehereden softly. 'Too late for you to come back to us, to come back to *me*.' Heat surged and Ataghan scrambled up, already reaching for his knife. 'Don't,' said Sehereden, but Ataghan strode away into the darkness.

They rode in silence the next day but as Esh-accom's wall came into sight, Ataghan let Taris have his head. The big stallion stretched out in a hard gallop and Ataghan urged him on, aware that Sehereden's stallion Fara galloped at his shoulder. The rough ground made their speed dangerous but Sehereden gave a whoop and Ataghan joined in, reminded of other wild rides they had shared.

But even as they neared the wall, another rider galloped out to meet them and, as the distance narrowed, Ataghan saw it was Brithergen. He ordered Taris to slow but the big stallion's blood was up and they all but overshot each other. The three horses came together in a rearing, stamping mass, but Ataghan barely noticed. Brithergen meeting them beyond the gate could not possibly be good news and yet the old warrior's face was all but split in two by a gigantic grin.

He reached over and gripped Ataghan's arm. 'We've got Fariye,' he said. 'She's unharmed.'

Ataghan had no memory of the gallop to the wall, of passing through the gate, of the crowd that had gathered. All he saw was what he had never thought to see again: Fariye's perfect face as she waited with his men. Then she was in his arms, her small body pressed against his.

Somewhere further off there was cheering and the sound of Sehereden's voice as he cleared a way through the crowd, then he was in the small room where the Wall Guard slept, alone with the child he had thought dead.

She clung to him and cried but interspersed with her sobs was a desperate pleading. 'You have to get her back, da. The bad men took her. You have to get her back. She's my lein, da. You have to get her back.'

He disengaged her arms, so he could see her tear-stained face. 'Who Fariye? Who do I have to get back?'

'Viv.'

Chapter 14

Ataghan and Sehereden spoke long into the night, their voices low for Fariye slept nearby, curled in Ataghan's bed. She had given a stumbling account of the attack on Esh-embrin and of her meeting and travels with Viv, but the story was full of gaping holes. Ataghan had not pressed her about Esh-embrin, he could well imagine the horrors she had witnessed there, but he did about Viv's dealings with the Scharii, and about the Waradi tryst-bracelet.

It was obvious the Scharii distrusted Viv, although there was nothing remarkable in that, distrust of elddra was widespread, but Viv's explanation of having taken the bracelet from the Lefer was ludicrous.

Fariye continued to insist Viv was not lein-trysted to a Waradi but was mystified by the Waradi mug in the makeshift food sling. They did not have anything to carry water, she said, but it also emerged she had been ill for a time and had vague memories of a cave.

'The elddra obviously re-joined her lover there,' said Ataghan.

'But to what purpose?' said Sehereden. 'None of it makes sense. If she knew who Fariye was and only cared for her to bargain with us later, she would have done so when we caught her.' His face hardened. 'We'll never know what her motives were.'

'I'm going back for her.'

Sehereden looked at him in shock. 'They would have entered the Grey Fire days ago! She's dead, At, and if you follow her, you'll die too.' His voice sank to a harsh whisper. 'If *my* love can't hold you here, Fariye's should. She needs you more than ever now.'

'The woman's elddra, Sehereden.'

'Only Stonash and urrut survive the Grey Fire!'

'I survived.'

Sehereden's hand fastened on his arm. 'Enda won't grant you that grace a second time! And even if the elddra survives, she'll be disfigured. Those the Grey Fire burns don't *want* to live.'

'*I* healed.'

'You had urrut fat and fleeces, she has nothing!'

Ataghan placed his hand over his lein's. 'I can't return her amé, Sehereden, so I'll repay my debt by giving her mine. If nothing else, my daughter's protector will have a safe journey through death.'

Ataghan was gone by dawn having collected fleeces, urrut fat, black-bor and hareesh, and visited Matharen, the most senior of the Sylds, to formalise the passing of his choose-daughter to Sehereden, should he not return. He did not tell the Syld what he intended or wait for Fariye to wake, and so it fell to Sehereden to tell her the father she had finally found, had disappeared from her life again.

'But he's gone to get Viv, hasn't he, Ser?' the little girl mumbled, still drowsed with sleep.

Sehereden settled on the edge of the bed. 'He's gone to *look* for her, Fari, but he mightn't find her,' he said gently. 'There's fighting in the vals.'

'Da will find her and then I'll have my lein back,' insisted Fariye, but her lip trembled and

Sehereden gathered her into his arms, as he had countless times before. They would be unlikely even to get her da's body back, he thought grimly.

'Did Viv suggest the leinship or did you?' he asked to distract her.

'I did. Viv didn't know about leinships or lots of other things.'

Sehereden frowned. 'Such as?'

'Oh, that you could eat black-bor, that oilstone starts fires, that only vals have rills, the colour of Eshadi horses, the—'

'The colour of Eshadi horses?' he said sharply.

'She didn't even know ours are dark grey with silver manes and tails.'

Sehereden's mind raced. They had dyed their mounts' manes and tails to disguise their Eshadi origins when crossing into Ascavale. If Viv had not recognised them as Eshadi, his claim she had no interest in using Fariye as a bargaining chip, might be wrong. 'Did she say which val she grew up in?' he asked.

'She said she didn't come from the vals. She's Astraali.'

'She *said* that?'

Sehereden had never known an elddra to volunteer her lineage and for the first time Poss hesitated. 'She said she didn't come from there either, but she must have, mustn't she, Ser?'

'If she lied about that, she might have lied about other things, Fari,' he said gently, although like so much else about her, the lie made no sense. Her looks marked her as Astraali seed as surely as a horse's colouring marked their Vale and yet, he had never known an elddra to have such eyes. They were almost violet.

'She said she wasn't Astraali because she knew da wouldn't want her with me, but he'll let her stay, won't he, Ser? Viv looked after me when she was scared too, and when the bad men came, she led them away.'

83

'Maybe she simply re-joined them,' said Sehereden. 'She had a Waradi tryst-bracelet, Fari, *and* a Waradi mug.' His words were brutal, but he needed to discover *what* Viv was.

'She's *not* with them!' said Fariye fiercely. 'Viv said not to move, but I saw what they did!' Fariye panted as if she had run and Sehereden held her close again and recalled how the elddra had screamed when he had held *her* close. Sehereden's face hardened. Valen customs varied but it was always the woman's choice who she coupled with or not and *never* the man's.

After they had breakfasted, Sehereden took Fariye down to the wrights who traded near Axian. She had been found within sight of the wall, and been bathed and dressed in clean clothes, but they were worn, and Ataghan would not approve. But Sehereden mainly wanted to take Fariye's mind off her missing lein *and* off her da too. She loved the trinkets Ataghan brought with him when he returned to the Scinta-ril and Sehereden wanted to see that happy smile again.

She clung to his hand as they made their way down the back streets and Sehereden chose the confectioners as their first stop. He let her choose her favourite shallit and traded kaest brittle for himself. The streets around Axian were almost as busy as Fire Zadic, with Valen forced from their homes by the fighting joining Esh-accom's traders.

Goods flowed from the vals up to the Astraali city, and back the other way. Urrut fleece, hides, horn, bone, smoked meat, cheese, kaest nuts and oil, bolts of cloth, raw leather, soap, perfumes, wood and metal implements were all taken by the Stonash along the crests, through the Grey Fire and endless ice ridges, to the city in the clouds, and beautifully worked silver and gemmed mirrors, candle sticks, lamps, jewellery, finely woven fabrics, ornate ceramics, and the trinkets beloved by Fariye were carried back.

Fariye's excitement grew as they passed stalls filled with enamel-ware and glass, and Sehereden's worry eased. The leather-wright had shoes Sehereden had never seen before and, although the blue patterned leather she chose was less robust than her boots, he let her have them.

'Now I'm like Sindarella,' she sang, as she danced out of the stall.

'*Sindarella*?' he asked and was treated to a long and breathless story. 'I've not heard that tale before,' he said, when she had finished.

'It's one of Viv's,' said Fariye. 'I lost my shoe at Esh-embrin and Sindarella lost *her* shoe. Viv carried me for ages then she made me a shoe out of her shirt. She was cold afterwards, so when we reached our sett, she took a jacket from the store.'

'You told your da that?' asked Sehereden. Ataghan had recognised the jacket as from his val but if he had also recognised it as Fariye's *mother's*, it might explain the depth of his antagonism for the elddra.

'I told da Viv took me to our sett, but it was burned, and about the Scharii hurting her.'

Ataghan had not told him the sett had gone nor about the Scharii, but Sehereden did not press Fariye with questions, and nor did he need to. Fariye became increasingly talkative as their expedition continued and the more he learned, the more mystified he grew. Nothing about Viv, or *Violet Iris Vacia*, made sense, including her peculiar name, but the odds were shortening his lein had condemned his daughter's saviour to death.

He managed to keep up a cheerful patter of conversation as they navigated their way to the cloth-wright Brithergen's si-tryst had recommended and when Fariye's mouth formed a circle, he knew he was in for a long wait. The cloth-wright directed him to a seat outside and once the man had ushered Fariye away through the bright rows of tunics and trousers, Sehereden could let the happy expression slide from his face. At least his vantage point offered some distractions from his thoughts, he comforted himself.

He had known those of Ataghan's sett since the leinship but the Valen here were strangers and seemed almost as exotic as the Astraali. Women strolled by clad in glittering fabrics, their dark eyes holding his, and the passing men appraised him too, as he appraised them. Cascade Zadic marked the start of a woman's journey to atunement and it was an advantage to be in Esh-accom as early as possible.

He benefitted from the leinship too. The trial tournaments might be many days away but the excitement of those who had seen Ataghan compete last zadican drew attention to Sehereden too. He had heard Ataghan's name whispered as he moved about Esh-accom but also anxious mutterings the fighting might disrupt the festivities. The tournaments attracted traders from far flung vals who left Esh-accom far richer than when they arrived, especially Esh-accom's Sylds.

The fighting was remote for those who had lost nothing and no one but for those who had lost everything, Esh-accom's very walls seemed threatened. They poured into Esh-accom with troubling tales of how dangerous it was to travel the vals, and news of Esh-min's devastation had spread too, seeding a taste for revenge. The Eshadi fought in bands with a discipline imposed by the leader, and it did not augur well for peace if mobs rode out intent on settling blood-debts.

Sehereden took a deep breath and forced his attention back to the crowd in time to see two elddra. Their auburn hair was streaked with grey which made them very old, given they aged more slowly than Valen, and their discomfort at being confined among the Valen was obvious. The crowd parted to let them through, Eshaccom's citizens less suspicious of strangers than Valen from the smaller setts. Trade brought the Stonash within the walls, and even their kin the Long-arms, and the tournament's festivities attracted those whose dress and customs were very different.

The elddra had no interest in trade, and certainly none in tournaments and festivities, and Sehereden guessed they sort protection from the fighting. His thoughts returned to Viv and then one of the elddra turned and met his eyes. He had a distinct feeling she was interested in him too, *because of Viv*, and then the crowd thickened and he lost sight of them.

The cloth-wright appeared and summoned him, and Fariye excitedly showed him the clothing she had chosen. There was a new set for her lein too, she told him excitedly, and Sehereden looked at them to ensure they would fit, in the unlikely event the elddra survived, silently handed over the traders, and tucked the bundle of clothing under his arm.

'We need to find a metal-wright now,' said Fariye, peering up and down the street.

'Why?'

'To get Viv an amé casque. She only had a piece of cloth to protect her amé.'

Sehereden forced a smile. 'That can wait,' he said and took her hand. 'Let's see what we can find to eat. You can choose today, and I'll choose tomorrow, or you can tell Mereya what you'd like.'

Mereya looked after Ataghan's compound in Esh-accom and readied it for his visits, and she looked after Fariye too on the rare occasions Ataghan brought her with him. Sehereden steered Fariye towards a tavern with just a few tables inside. It suited Sehereden who much preferred the Scinta-ril's quiet to Esh-accom's noise.

Fariye chose meatballs spiced with issen, and retsen bread and honey, a rather plain choice, but one Sehereden was happy to share. He found the taverns' food in Esh-accom either too peppery or too greasy, and to make matters worse, they doused their red-roots and ardins in urrut butter.

Sehereden settled Fariye at a table and struck up a conversation with the tavern-keeper as he laboured at his stove. The man was happy to chat and knowing who Sehereden was, soon repeated the widespread hope the Sylds would put things to rights in the vals. Sehereden nodded noncommittedly and steered the conversation to the elddra he had seen, and how they, along with the many others who sought sanctuary in Esh-accom, could be accommodated.

There was ample space for everyone, the tavern-keeper assured him, even the elddra. Unlike most of those who flooded in from the vals, they preferred the Old Quarter, where it was quieter and where the older buildings attracted little competition from others seeking lodging.

Chapter 15

Sehereden insisted Fariye rest when they returned to the compound. He knew she had been ill on her trek with the elddra, and her face still showed moments of bleakness from her ordeal at Esh-embrin. He let her use Ataghan's bed, instead of her own, and she hugged one of his pillows as she curled up. 'They'll be back soon, won't they, Ser?'

'It's a long journey, Fari,' he said, and kissed her forehead. 'Sleep.'

'You won't go away too, will you?'

'I'll be here, Fariye, I promise.'

She slept then, and Sehereden leaned back in his chair and watched her. Ataghan had never lied to Fariye about anything, even her mother, and Sehereden was not about to start now. It meant future conversations were going to be brutal but at least he had time on his side. Even if Enda granted a miracle and Ataghan survived to retrieve a living elddra, the soonest he could return was late in Cascade. But Sehereden was not betting on miracles and that meant he had half a zadic to somehow prepare Fariye for the loss of her lein *and* her da.

It was mid-afternoon before Sehereden set out with Fariye for Brithergen's compound. It lay close to the Old Quarter, which was convenient, although not the reason he went there. Many of Brithergen's kin made Esh-accom their home and his compound included children.

Sehereden had arranged for Fariye to spend the night there and she chattered excitedly as they walked. Apart from children, the compound included si-trysts and even lein-trysts, who would help Fariye heal. It would take time

89

to rebuild the sett at Scinta-ril and longer still to build a community. But Ataghan's band would return there with new si- and lein-trysts and choose- and seed-children, and those attracted by At's triumphs in the tournaments. It would be a place of happiness again, he reassured himself.

Ataghan had expected trouble, but no one had predicted the Ascadi would join the attacks. Once they followed the Waradi over the crests, setts became death-traps, and the Eshadi were now beset sunwise *and* nightwise. The Eshadi Sylds had received no offers of help from Vales cloudwise of the Ascadi and Waradi, but any Beshadi or Genessi messengers sent by *their* Sylds must first cross the Ascadi and Waradi's murderous Vales and might not have survived.

Sehereden did not delay long after exchanging pleasantries with Brithergen and his si-tryst Loreya. Like the rest of the band, Brithergen knew Ataghan was absent, and Sehereden let them assume his lein hunted the Waradi leader alone despite it galling him.

He gave Fariye a final hug then made his way into the Old Quarter and down its narrow streets until the clang of beaten metal heralded the metal-wrights. He wanted trinkets for Fariye but he needed gifts for the elddra too. Choosing a selection of dainty enamelled flowers for Fariye was easy, but not the second trade. The elddra admired silverware but he did not want the gift to be seen as a bribe. Whatever the Valen muttered about the elddra's arrogant Astraali blood, he was keen not to insult them.

He settled on two silver hand mirrors of Astraali workmanship, with a single angellus wing engraved on the back so that when they were laid side by side, the mirrors formed a pair. He hoped the reference to the Angellus would please them but as he went on, he recollected that the elddra rarely acknowledged their origins. He shrugged. He no idea why he wasted his time trying to solve the mystery of a *dead* elddra anyway.

Before he left the last of the metal-wrights behind, he also traded for several charm-chains and a dozen exquisitely wrought tribute-charms of flowers, stars, and birds. He would need them during Fire Zadic *if* he were not in some far flung val fighting for his life.

The Old Quarter was as tangled as the Leferen's waste-wood and he had to stop several times to orientate himself. It would be pointless asking directions at one of the taverns he passed for the elddra ate only rarely, and in the end, he turned down an alleyway simply to escape the crowds. It was quiet and its close-set walls made it cool but as his footsteps rasped along, he wondered whether it led anywhere at all.

It did, finally delivering him to an expanse of moss-covered paving. Leaves blew in lazy circles and he looked up, astonished to see koachars, though whoever had planted the giants had realised their mistake and lopped the tops off. It was surprisingly quiet, given Esh-accom's bustle, but he heard the sound of water and saw that a fountain sparkled in the sunshine.

A small statue of an Angellus had been fixed in the centre of a shallow bowl and the whole lot set upon an ornamental pedestal. The Angellus's wings had been broken off and it held some sort of musical instrument that was also broken. Flakes of blue and white paint clung to the figure, but most of it had been washed away by the water that bubbled from the figure's head. The bowl's rim seemed badly chipped too, but closer inspection revealed it depicted the mountains that rimmed Astraal's sacred lake.

'I see you admire the *Fountain of the Angellus*, lein of Ataghan en-Scinta-ril,' a voice behind him said.

Sehereden turned. A woman sat on a stone bench in the koachar's shade, her sewing-work on her lap, her basket beside her. Sehereden gave the bow customary to greeting a woman, known or unknown, and settled on the bench at a polite distance. 'It was obviously constructed before the Astraali became less admired,' he said, his gaze on the fountain.

'It was constructed in memory of the *Angellus*.'

'Same thing,' he said, with a shrug.

'They are very different things,' she corrected. 'The Angellus have long since departed, and those who remain are but *part* Angellus. They took the name Astraali to differentiate themselves, and changed Ourassin's name to Astraal, to tighten their claim on the peak.'

Sehereden looked at her in surprise. 'You're wondering why my version of events contradicts the Valens', Ataghan en-Scinta-ril's lein?' she asked with a smile. 'I am Mareva en-Thinda-ril and a cloth-wright, as you see, and no scholar.' Sehereden held his tongue and her smile broadened. 'You've more patience than your lein but I suspect your curiosity is no less. Those who flee the fighting must often leave their possessions behind and so there's demand for a trade such as mine, even from elddra.'

Still Sehereden said nothing, and she eyed him speculatively. 'It's known in Esh-accom, that the appearance of your lein's choose-daughter, when even your lein thought her dead, owes much to an elddra. There are many who are curious about this elddra, including the elddra themselves, for whom I presently sew.'

'Ah,' said Sehereden.

'The elddra hold us in the same regard as we hold them and prefer their own company,' went on Mareva candidly, 'even so, I find them easier to trade with than Valen. They're not given to dispute, except over *our* version of their history.'

'I suppose they're entitled to be, given it's *their* history,' conceded Sehereden and glanced back at the fountain. 'It would be useful to meet with these elddra. While my lein has learned some things from his choose-daughter, I would like to provide him with a fuller account on his return.'

Mareva nodded. 'Their compound is close,' she said, and gave him directions.

'I thank you,' he said, bowed again, and set off.

Chapter 16

The building looked the same as its neighbours, with rendered walls yellowed with age and shutters in need of another coat of oil. He knocked on the door and waited, and was considering knocking again, when the door opened. It was one of the elddra he had seen earlier, and he stepped back and bowed, keen to be courteous.

'The lein of Ataghan en-Scinta-ril,' the elddra said, her pale eyes holding his. 'What brings you to Esh-accom's *poorer quarter*?'

'The wish for information,' he said, ignoring her mocking tone. Elddra did not flaunt their wealth but nor did they house themselves shabbily and it must aggravate them to be forced from their usual compounds. The elddra continued to scrutinise him and he gave an easy smile. 'As you may know, my lein's choose-daughter was cared for by an elddra. We would like to know more about her.'

'For what purpose?'

It was an obvious question and Sehereden did not dissemble. 'My lein's choose-daughter has sworn leinship with her. As you can appreciate, this is a serious matter.'

The elddra blinked in shock. 'I am Anetherey,' she said, and beckoned him in. Sehereden followed her down a hallway, irritated she had not revealed her rill despite knowing his, and they entered a small light-filled room. The second elddra sat there at a table laden with scroll casques and Sehereden bowed again.

The lack of introductions told him she was the more senior of the two and he waited while Anetherey briefly related their conversation. The second elddra's eyes were pale like her companion's but sheened amethyst in the light. 'Be seated, *Ataghan's* lein,' she said.

Sehereden was used to being addressed by his lein's title, but there was something about the way the elddra said it, that put him on edge. Her pale eyes regarded him for a moment. 'All elddra are known to each other, *Ataghan's* lein, yet this elddra is known to no one,' she said.

'Her name is Viv,' said Sehereden, taken aback by her bluntness.

'Which is not an elddra name.'

Sehereden had been unaware elddra names were distinct but hid his surprise. 'Nor a Valen one,' he said smoothly. 'She told me it was formed from the initial letters of three other names: Violet, Iris, Vacia.'

'You have met her?' asked the elddra sharply.

'Yes.'

'Where is she now?'

'I can't tell you.'

The elddra considered him for a moment. 'You have a lein, Sehereden en-Scinta-ril, who you would give your life for, and he for you, but the elddra have no need of such arrangements; our bloodline makes us one.' She paused. 'And yet, we have more in common than you think. We both want information about this elddra, and we both have things we will not share. Do you agree?'

'Yes,' said Sehereden, again nonplussed by her directness.

'You have the advantage of having seen her. Describe her to me.'

'She's about your height, is slender, and has short dark red curls.'

'And her age?'

Sehereden shrugged. 'She *looks* young but it's hard for Valen to judge the age of elddra,' he admitted.

'Our eyes lighten with age.'

'Then she's *very* young. Her eyes are almost purple.' Anetherey's breath hissed, and Sehereden saw the senior elddra's quick warning glance. 'She denied being from the vals *or* from Astraal,' he added, his attention now on Anetherey. 'Yet elddra claim not to lie.'

'I cannot speak on behalf of *this* elddra,' the more senior elddra said.

Anetherey had managed to calm and Sehereden shifted his attention back to the senior elddra. She had avoided his question about elddra deceit, but his thoughts had turned to the Waradi leader. 'Is it common for elddra to lein-tryst with Valen?' he asked.

'Elddra do not lein-tryst with Valen,' the senior elddra said coolly. 'They cannot meet our needs.'

The answer was insulting, as if Valen men, him included, lacked the skills to deliver sexual pleasure. 'Elddra don't risk their lives for Valen children either,' he retorted, 'yet she risked herself more than once for my lein's choose-daughter.'

'You imply this elddra was alone before she came upon the child,' the elddra said, ignoring his outburst.

'She *was* alone.'

'Elddra do not travel alone, *Ataghan's* lein. Could her companion have remained hidden?'

'Not an *elddra* companion,' he said, his thoughts on the Waradi again.

The elddra paused, as if she sifted the implications of other types of companions. 'Is there anything else you can tell me?' she asked.

'Not without something more in return.'

'We are both constrained in our own ways,' she conceded, 'but I will say this: the elddra of whom we speak is important to us.' She paused then seemed to come to a decision. 'There is an elddra permitted to speak more freely than I, but she will require you to speak more freely in return. She resides at the Bracken-ril. If you visit her, you may say you have spoken with Anfarena.'

'I will think on it,' said Sehereden and bowed to mask his astonishment. In revealing her name, the senior elddra had revealed just how keen she was to discover Viv's identity, and that added a whole new layer to the mystery.

He took the mirrors from his jacket pocket and placed them on the table. 'Please accept these as a gesture of my lein's and my goodwill. The elddra saved the life of my lein's choose-child and is important to us as well.'

Sehereden slept little that night as he trawled through the exchange. Anetherey's shock at Viv's eye-colour made him wonder whether eye-colour denoted more than age, but if so, what? He next considered Anfarena's assertion that elddra did not travel alone. His lein believed Viv travelled with the Waradi leader, but if so, her care of Fariye and everything else that had followed, made no sense. It also contradicted Anfarena's dismissal of elddra-Valen lein-trysts.

And then there was the leinship. Anetherey had been shocked when he had mentioned the elddra's leinship with Fariye and now Sehereden saw why. Anfarena, clearly the elddra in charge, implied that elddra scorned such arrangements. *Our bloodline makes us one,* she had said.

Sehereden swore softly. He had gone to the elddra for answers and come away with more questions. *If* the name Viv was not an elddra one and she was not known to the elddra, who apparently knew *all* their kind, and *if* she travelled alone and had sworn a leinship with Fariye, when elddra spurned leinships, and *if* she denied being from Astraal, then maybe she was not elddra at all.

It was possible that chance had produced a Valen woman with the slightness, hair colour, and purple-blue eyes of an elddra, but she had not denied being elddra when he and At had called her elddra, she had only denied it to Fariye, along with being born in either Astraal or the Vales, or so Fariye said.

Maybe Fariye was confused, or maybe the elddra *was* a liar. Anfarena had refused to deny or confirm that particular fact, but she had given him the chance to find out more, *if* he chose. *There is an elddra permitted to speak more freely than I,* she said but of course, it had not been anywhere close-by.

Bracken-ril was in icestone country, where sliding stone buried a man in the blink of an eye. It was a dangerous journey at the best of times, and these were not the best of times. Apart from anything else, risking his life going to Bracken-ril risked his pledge to care for Fariye, because if both he and Ataghan died, Fariye would have no one.

And yet, despite everything, he did not entirely dismiss the idea of seeking out Bracken-ril's elddra. There would be time enough later, he concluded grimly, when his lein *did not* return, to finally scour the possibility from his mind.

Sehereden collected Fariye from Brithergen's compound the following day, pleased by how happy she looked. He heard every detail of what she had eaten, the games of hide and chase she had played, and won, and how Brithergen had let her help at the stables. Sehereden thought being reminded of Sita might upset her, but there was only a momentary pause, before she returned to her favourite subject of her lein.

That suited Sehereden well. It was sometimes hard to sift useful information Fariye's chatter, but Viv's ignorance of the Vales was glaring. Even if she *had* been raised in isolation in some obscure val, she would have known how rills ran and oilstone worked.

'Did Viv say what she was doing near Esh-embrin?' he asked.

'Looking for her mother,' said Fariye promptly.

Sehereden's heart quickened as he recalled Anfarena's claim of elddra having companions. 'Was she with her mother before they got separated?'

'No, with Thris.'

'Thris?' repeated Sehereden nonplussed.

Fariye dropped her voice conspiratorially. 'I think Thris is her lein-tryst. She said he wasn't but you could tell when she was thinking about him.'

Sehereden rubbed his jaw as the mystery deepened. 'You met Thris?' he asked.

'Of course not. I would've told you. Viv said they were attacked and that's how they got separated. She woke up near Esh-embrin and found me in the cave. She said when I was safely back with da, she'd start looking for her mother again, but I want her to stay here. Da will let her stay, won't he, Ser? She's my lein.'

'You're very young to have lein,' he said, as gently as he could. 'And Viv being elddra complicates things.'

Fariye's chin came up. 'Viv sang to me in the cave near Esh-embrin and used her jacket to make me a shoe.

She carried me when I was sick and told me stories when I was frightened. She told me not to trust anyone, just like da, and even when the Scharii hurt her, she didn't blame me.'

Fariye's dark eyes came to his. 'When I was small, da told me what a leinship was, how you and da loved and trusted each other, and how that would never change. I love Viv and trust her, and that will never change. That's why she's my lein.'

Chapter 17

Ataghan rode hard for four days and only a stallion of Taris's strength could have endured it. Their shared link held the stallion to Ataghan's will and when he farewelled him, Ataghan touched his forehead to Taris's and instructed him to return to Esh-accom. Taris had been with Ataghan six zadicans and Ataghan might never see him again, but he wasted no time on regret just tightened his pack, turned upslope, and ran.

When he reached the ridge top he settled into a lope. Urrut dung told him the caravan was at least three days ahead, but once he reached the Grey Fire, he must catch it in two *or die*. He controlled his breathing and stride length to conserve his strength, and the day was less than half done when he heard the keening and stopped.

He lathered his face and hands with a thick layer of urrut fat, donned the fleece, and wrapped a strip around his face with a slit for his eyes. Then he looked back towards Esh-accom where his lein and choose-daughter dwelt, took a deep breath, and ran headlong into the howling.

It was as if he had jumped into a cauldron. His skin blistered and blood scoured his throat, but he ran on, calculating the distance between the oilstone caves he must use on his return to survive.

Day turned to night and back to day and Ataghan registered the change, despite the Grey Fire's undifferentiated murk. The ice-fire tore at his flesh, but he seemed removed from it, as if it happened to someone else. Another night slid past and then the smell of fresh dung penetrated his senses and consciousness stormed back bringing with it a horrendous pain.

Urrut rumps emerged from the gloom, massive mounds of lumbering flesh, bereft of any elddra companion. His pace took him in amongst them and he followed the leash deep into the urrut's coat. A single knife-stroke severed it, and a jerk yanked the body free. It fell to the ground and he dragged a fleece from his pack, rolled it around the body, heaved it over his shoulder, and ran back the way he had come.

He had no idea whether he carried a corpse or something living, and no time to find out. Its lightness suggested a corpse, for the Grey Fire desiccated rather than decayed. He came to the first of the oilstone caves, set the body down, and cracked oilstone with his heel. Flame blossomed, and more oilstone followed. Then he dragged the body close to the fire's roar, crouched beside it, and counted silently. When he reached fifty, he hauled the body back over his shoulder, and ran on.

In the second cave he counted to a hundred beside the fire, and in the third, he loosened the fleeces from the elddra's shoulders, and his own, to allow more heat to penetrate. Pain speared his chest but the elddra lay unmoving. Her red curls were the only thing he recognised, the skin of her face and shoulders as ridged as koachar bark, and too thick to find a pulse.

His face and hands were burned too but the fat had protected him from the worse of it. Even so, the Grey Fire had taken a horrendous toll and the only thing that propelled him forwards was the promise of rest at the next cave.

He was all but spent by the time he reached it and once the fire blazed, gulped down hareesh before he could shrug open his fleeces. Pain escalated as he warmed, and he struggled to unwrap the elddra. There was still nothing to show she lived but he heaved her onto his lap and up ended a hareesh flask into her mouth.

The stimulant trickled from her cracked lips and he grunted. The thickened skin made it hard for her to swallow but if she were to live, swallow she must. He tried again, with the same result, then took a swig, clamped his mouth over hers, and transferred it that way.

It was the least passionate kiss he had ever delivered but the hareesh did not leak back, not that it proved anything; it might have simply drained down a dead gullet. He continued to hold her, too exhausted to put her down, and sensed the slightest of movements, but there was nothing more.

One more dash would take him out of the Grey Fire, but he could scarcely move. He swigged down more hareesh and, grunting in pain, pulled his fleeces tight, re-wrapped the elddra, staggered upright and ran.

Later when he tried to recall that last desperate sprint, it was as if someone had scrubbed it from his mind. He could not even recollect the moment he had burst free from the appalling howling. When he came to his senses he was in a cave, next to a fire. At least he'd had the wits to unwrap himself *and* the elddra, so the fire warmth reached both their skins.

He took several more gulps of hareesh and pulled her onto his lap. Her clothes smelled of urrut but as he smoothed the hair from her ravaged face, a potent fragrance filled the air and something stirred, deep in his guts, and he wiped his hand on his trousers. He had coupled with women after tournaments who smelled similar, and he concluded her stinking Waradi lover had gifted her perfume.

He transferred another mouthful of hareesh and felt her swallow, but offered up no thanks to Enda, simply delivered several more mouthfuls then lay her next to the fire. Her head rolled from side to side, and he was glad he had kept her collared and leashed. He could not afford to waste his strength fighting her when he might have to fight others.

Viv's first awareness was of horrendous pain, of being jerked along over someone's shoulder, of bitter concoctions being forced down her throat. Swallowing was hard and opening her eyes harder and, as she became more lucid, the awful realisation dawned that her wooden face was not a dream. And then, as a ghastly finale, she realised the man who had her was the arsehole who had sent her into the ice-fire.

He brought his face close to hers and repeated the same phrases, but it took her a long time to understand what he said, and then she had called him a liar. There was no way this arsehole could have fathered Poss, and then her confusion dissipated, and everything became appallingly clear.

The man was called Ataghan and was Fariye's choose-father. Fariye was safe in Esh-accom and had told him of Viv's care. He had retrieved her to even the debt. The Grey Fire meant she was scarred for life, but his own skin would heal. The possibility of Ascadi or Waradi attack was real, and if she aided the enemy, he would kill her. And before he was done with her, she would tell him the truth.

Viv scarcely heard his threats, the single phrase *scarred for life*, reverberating in her head. She felt her face as she stumbled along, but her hands were the same ridged grey as the Stonash's, and she needed no mirror to know her face was the same.

There would be no escape through the nearest rift because any human caste fold would find her grotesque. There might be pity for her, but fear was more likely, and fear fed hatred and violence. Witch-burners had targeted the disfigured as well as the herb-wise.

And then the terrible realisation struck her there would be no more glorious love-making with Thris either, *or* quest to find her mother, and that Poss was lost to her too, the little girl having seen too much horror for Viv to inflict more.

The magnitude of what this man had robbed her of fed a hatred as corrosive as acid. She had never felt such loathing before, even for Jimmy Wright as he had beaten her mother, and she pledged she would kill this man, or see him killed, before she was done.

Ataghan wondered whether the elddra's submissiveness was a ruse but decided it was shock and considered his options if she slowed his journey. It had been a mistake to send Taris back to Esh-accom but the risk to the stallion from Waradi or Ascadi attack was too great to keep him close. He was in danger too given the treacherous elddra he kept company with could tip the balance in his enemies' favour in any fight.

Despite what he had told Sehereden, he had expected to find a corpse attached to the tether rope, discharge his debt via the pyre, then break the news to Fariye that her lein had perished, but the elddra had not perished and that created a problem.

He could not distress Fariye by taking her back to Esh-accom, where she would be shunned in any case, in fact, it was hard to think of anywhere she would not be shunned.

Even her beloved Waradi lein-tryst would spurn her.

But he was not about to turn her loose to stir up more trouble, and he dredged his memory for some far-flung val he could leave her. There was Tahsin en-Kama-ril's sett, he recalled, *if* the old Eshadi still lived. The sett was certainly isolated but produced high quality retsen and Ataghan had traded for it before. The elddra was light too, as were all her kind, which meant she could earn her keep in retsen harvest. She might even be a good fit for the sett. He recalled that Tahsin had a habit of collecting the bizarre and broken, almost as if the Valen misfits were pretty feathers.

But a detour to the Kama-ril would cost him time he did not have, not with the Waradi leader enjoying his freedom, and Ascadi bands roaming at will. His brows drew as he considered the quickest route and his ill temper grew as he realised it lay straight cloudwise through icestone country.

Yet it might be worth the risk to be able to tell Fariye the elddra lived but was too far away to visit. It also meant that with no contact between them, there was a good chance Fariye would forget she ever had a lein, and her life go on as before.

Chapter 18

Viv sat with her gaze on the new constellation. The previous one had been called Pool, but she had no idea what this one was called. Tarchen had mentioned one called Horse, and Poss had spoken of one called Fire, but whatever this one was, watching it was a million times better than watching the arsehole.

She could scarcely believe he was Poss's father, *choose*-father, she amended. Poss's love for him had been obvious but he had led a massacre then sent her into the ice-fire, and now he dragged her along on a leash. Maybe his brutality flowed from the drugs he was on, and he was different clean. *Yeah, sure Vivi, just like Jimmy Wright. He was a wonderful dad, wasn't he, when he wasn't boozed out of his brain.*

Viv grimaced but her face did not move. At least she no longer had to worry about revealing her feelings, she thought bitterly, unlike the arsehole, who actually looked worried. Considering how efficient he was at murdering, he probably was not fretting over someone sneaking up on them, not that there was anywhere for attackers to hide. The rubble was too loose for even plants or bushes to stay put, or the stone itself, with regular rumbles of it down the slopes to either side.

At least the new zadic gave them light to travel by, and she guessed the arsehole had stopped to wait for it. He did not look tired or hungry, and when she ignored his offer of water and blackbor, he had not eaten either.

The gang's addicts had preferred drugs to food, and she had learned to steer clear of the gang's more emaciated

107

members. The arsehole was not emaciated though, he was a ball of muscle. 'Time to go,' he said.

He tossed the food and flask into his pack and they went on. It looked like he intended to go straight over the head of the valley, but God only knew how. The ridge looked as stable as a stack of pebbles and a hell of a lot higher. A rill seeped from its base with no obvious streambed and cavernous pits opened to their left and right as they climbed. Something glimmered in their depths and after a while she realised they were bones.

'Fall in there, elddra, and that's where you'll stay,' said the arsehole. 'Not even maragh get out.' The arsehole's pace increased, and she stumbled, sending stones sliding behind them. 'Take care,' he snapped as he grabbed her wrist to steady her.

'Don't touch me, arsehole!' exclaimed Viv, jerking free.

He used the leash to reel her in like a fish. 'Learn some manners, elddra. My name's Ataghan and *I'll* decide what I'll do and not do.'

'That's what all addicts think,' she sneered, straining away from him. 'But it's the crap you're on that decides. Get off it, *arsehole*, for your daughter's sake.'

'*My* daughter's no concern of yours, elddra.'

'And no concern of yours either, given you left her unprotected!'

He jerked the leash until her face all but touched his but before he could speak, there was a grating sound, and he pushed her down. 'Jump when I tell you,' he ordered.

Viv's heart pounded as grit rained in stinging showers, but the avalanche slewed sideways before it reached them, and ended up in the pit to their right. The slurry triggered more slides down the pit's sides, and it was a long time before the rattle quieted, and he rose. 'The icestone—' he began, and then a final chunk of rock hurtled from the gloom, there was a sickening thud, and she was alone.

Viv stared about in astonishment, then crawled to the edge of the pit and peered in. The arsehole lay at the bottom, face up, blood on his brow. Their eyes met and then his head rolled side-ways and he was still. There lay the Waradi rapist, the loveless Jimmy Wright, the treacherous Kald, *and* every other violent thug she had fallen foul of.

She scrambled upright, grabbed a boulder, and with a howl of fury, raised it above her head. Then a constellation flashed into being, more brilliant than the others, *and* more fleeting. The boulder slipped from her nerveless hands and she sat clumsily. She felt tired suddenly, as if she had been in a long struggle. The constellation remained, not in the sky, but imprinted on her lids: an owl, picked out in stars.

She had loved their haunting calls as a child but now she loved their wings, because wings could lift you high above the world's ugliness, free you from your crappy human part, and wrap you in star-bursts of love and beauty.

Viv took a shuddering breath. She had once got into a car full of druggies and a child had died, and now she held another child's fate in her hands, a little girl who loved the man at the bottom of the pit.

She shed her shirt and jacket, unbedded her wings, and leapt skywards. It no longer mattered her face was a rucked mask or about the men who had damaged her in other ways. She was an angel, as free as they were, and just as wondrous in her perfection.

All she wanted to do was fly away, but she descended into the pit. The arsehole breathed but was half buried in stone and freeing him was like digging in dry sand. The real problem though was in getting him out of the pit.

She retrieved her jacket and knotted the sleeves under his arms, but even though he was lighter than his muscularity suggested, she was not strong enough to lift him clear of the ground.

The pit walls were in constant motion and she wondered if the stone's slipperiness could actually aid her. If she hovered above and dragged him, she might be able to *slide* him up the pit's sides. It was hard going but, bit by bit, she hauled him up and over the lip, then clear of the pit's crumbling edges.

She let her breathing steady, then dressed and used one of the arsehole's knives to cut off the collar and leash. She was tempted to hurl them into the pit but stuffed them in her pocket instead. A little reminder, she told herself grimly, to never put herself in the arsehole's power again.

His face was bloody, and she used his water flask to wash the gash. His greasy skin told her he had used something to protect himself from the ice-fire and hatred flared anew. Thris had taught her how damaging such emotions were and she struggled to calm long enough to check him for broken bones. Everything seemed intact, but his uneven breathing worried her, and she rolled him onto his side and tucked a fleece from his pack over him. His breathing slowly settled, and, despite her antagonism, Viv's tension eased too.

The slope still loomed above them and there was no guarantee their next attempt at it would be any better. She settled on a flat stone and lay her head on her knees. The night dragged on, made longer by the failure of the owl constellation to reappear, and she was glad when a slice of cool brightness heralded the dawn. Shit! It rose to her right! They headed north, the opposite direction to Esh-accom and Poss!

Viv glared down at the arsehole. He had made no secret of wanting the despised elddra out of his daughter's life and Viv felt the same way, but for very different reasons. Screaming at Poss to stay put while Viv ran for her life was not the way she wanted to part. She needed to tell Poss she loved her, and would never forget her, not just disappear like her own mother had.

So, if they were not heading to Esh-accom, where were they heading? To a people even more callous than the Stonash? Perhaps she should fly away after all, but where to? There would be no welcome in any human caste fold. And yet, as the new sun doused the slope in golden light, hope stirred. Her angel blood had healed her before, even after Rim's worst attack when, high as a kite, he had cornered her with a cigarette lighter, and she had to believe she would heal again *and* give Poss one last hug.

Chapter 19

Ataghan woke with a start, snatched his knives, and rolled into a crouch. His head pounded but he remained poised for battle. The slopes were bare of everything except the elddra, and he sheathed his knives. His throbbing head confirmed his last memory of being at the bottom of the pit, but he was not there now, and even the smallest Eshadi child knew nothing escaped their stinking walls. To add to the bizarreness, the elddra had not fled. 'I thought you would be long gone,' he said.

'Where?'

Her contempt told him nothing and he trawled through his pack for hareesh and took a swig. His head cleared a little and he noticed the fleece at his feet and recalled it had been tucked over him. 'How did you get me out the pit?' he demanded.

'I sprouted wings.'

Her sarcasm grated but he had a more pressing question. 'Why bother?'

'Your daughter needs you.' She had used his knife to cut off the collar and leash, he noticed, and he could probably thank Fariye she had not slit his throat as well. He considered binding her again but did not think she would fight him, for Fariye's sake, and the icestone reduced the risk of attack. Even the Waradi had the sense to keep well clear of it.

The climb was perilous, but they reached the ridge top without further mishap. The elddra asked for no food, water or rest which quickened their pace but her loathing of him was palpable. He did not dwell on it. There was a price for trysting with an enemy who murdered women, children, and the old, and she was fortunate the price had not been her life.

The elddra walked in silence but she scanned as much as he did, and his tension built. There were few hiding places on the barren slopes but many in the Kama-ril and given he must sleep for a short time, it would be better here, where attack was less likely.

'I need to rest for a time,' he said to her, as dusk neared. 'If your lein-tryst is close, be assured he will die here. And don't think I have forgotten, elddra, how much you've still to tell me about him.' She did not deign to answer, and he chose a place with stone at his back, unsheathed his knives, and let his eyelids close.

The Cascade's blaze woke him, and he rolled up into his habitual defensive position and, finding no threat, sheathed his knives. He had slept longer than intended, but the throb in his head had gone. The elddra sat nearby, her gaze on the stars and, as the zadic lit her profile, he sourly considered her Astraali father.

He would be Du-Daimon, given her youth, but the cloud-crawlers were all the same, despite their varying claims to the Angellus's purity. Her father had obviously been on poor terms with her mother, given she had left and taken her daughter with her. The Astraali would have been most *displeased*. They filled their compounds with the finest of everything, including the Valen's most beautiful women *and* their part-Astraali daughters. Ataghan's lip curled. But not their sons!

They went on, crossing the last of the icestone ridges by the Cascade's light and reaching the Kama-ril forests as it faded. Ataghan's mood lifted as the stone gave way to the moist softness of leaf-fall, and he calculated he should be at Tahsin's sett by dusk, and then, if things went well, on his way back to Fariye and Sehereden at dawn.

He ordered the elddra to walk beside him to prevent her signalling any enemies and as she came level, he smelled the sweetness again. He wondered what else apart from perfume the Waradi had gifted to win an elddra lein-tryst. She had worn a finely crafted tryst-bracelet but no necklets or rings, and her amé casque had been shabby. Ataghan's mouth twisted. The Waradi's sexual prowess had obviously been enough to keep her by his side!

Viv disliked the trees even more than the sliding stone because their trunks hid attackers and their branches blocked skyward escape. The arsehole was tense too, because he carried his knives, but he set a quick pace which told her he knew exactly where he headed. It was close to dusk again when she smelled smoke, but the arsehole showed no signs of alarm which meant the smoke came from their destination.

A yellow glow appeared through the trees then the dark outlines of buildings, and more blotches of yellow where light spilled from windows. The arsehole stopped and pulled material from his pack. 'It would be best if you covered your face,' he said. Best for *him*, perhaps, thought Viv savagely, making no move to take it. Why should *she* hide as if *she* were the criminal? 'Please yourself,' he said and then seized her arm and marched her forward.

'Let go of me, arsehole,' she hissed, struggling in his grip. Someone shouted a challenge and she wrenched herself free as a man loomed from the trees and a lamp was thrust in the arsehole's face. The arsehole went through his long-winded name and then it was her turn to be blinded by the light. Viv refused to say anything or drop her head and there was a short silence while the lamp-holder examined her, and then the lamp swung away.

'Tahsin eats,' the man said. 'Come, Tahsin will welcome you to his sett.'

The lamp's glare reduced the man to a massive silhouette and the arsehole grabbed her arm again and propelled her towards the building. Viv dreaded being thrust in front of so many people, but the arsehole dragged her in. The bright light blinded her, but there was warmth there too, the smell of food, and a sudden silence. Every face turned in their direction, but Viv kept her gaze straight ahead.

A man with a weather-beaten face and wild mop of grizzled hair rose from one of the tables. 'Ataghan en-Scinta-ril, welcome!' he boomed across the room. 'And welcome to you too, elddra. Welcome to Tahsin's sett. What are you named?'

'Viv.' She had to call her name back and realised the old man ensured everyone there knew she *had* a name but the way the arsehole hauled her across the room made her status as prisoner clear.

The people at Tahsin's table shuffled along to make room on the bench, and they sat down opposite the old man. Bowls of thick broth were set in front of them and small rounds of flat bread that still steamed from the oven. The doughy smell reminded Viv of the Keeper's house in Hearth Fold and she clenched her jaw.

115

'Eat,' said Tahsin, almost as loudly as when he had bawled across the room. 'Even elddra break their fast for Tahsin's *gorash*.'

'It's Prenya's gorash,' a gruff voice corrected to Viv's left. The speaker was a square-jawed woman with close-cropped hair. 'And the retsen's Borish's.'

'You're correct, Enesha, but I claim ownership as head of the sett,' said Tahsin good-naturedly. 'Eat,' he repeated, more softly to Viv. 'Elddra need food sometimes.' Viv picked up the spoon and took a mouthful of broth. It tasted like those her mother made when money was tight, but there was plenty of it. Her stiff lips made eating difficult, and she took care not to dribble.

'And what are you doing in the cloudwise vals, Viv?' asked Tahsin.

'Looking for my mother,' said Viv, knowing the arsehole listened, as did those nearby.

'How long since you saw her?'

'I was ten,' said Viv hoping to hide her ignorance of Valen time divisions.

'And now?'

'I'm eighteen.'

'Eight zadicans,' the old man said thoughtfully. 'That's a long time to be alone.'

'She has a Waradi lein-tryst to comfort her,' said the arsehole loudly. Viv sensed the tension in the room rise and tightened her grip on the spoon. The arsehole obviously intended to make her time here as miserable as possible.

'*Do* you have a Waradi lein-tryst?' asked Tahsin.

His face was almost as rucked as hers, but his dark eyes were not unkind. 'No.'

The arsehole grunted but Tahsin grinned, and Viv saw he did not have many teeth left. 'A difference of opinion between Ataghan en-Scinta-ril and Viv en-elddra,' he said jovially, then sobered. 'Ataghan en-Scinta-ril,' he said formally. 'Am I correct in supposing you want my sett to accept Viv en-elddra?'

'You are, Tahsin en-Kama-ril.'

'And what of your wants, Viv en-elddra?' asked Tahsin, turning his craggy face back to her. 'You're welcome here but everyone you see works to put the food you eat on the table, whether it be Prenya's, Borish's, or mine,' he added dryly. 'Will you work for my sett?'

'Yes, for as long as I'm here.'

Tahsin nodded and turned to the square-jawed woman to Viv's left. 'Enesha, Viv can have the room next to yours. Take her there and make sure she has what she needs. There are clothes that should fit her in the store. We'll look at the roster in the morning.'

Enesha rose but as Viv went to follow, the arsehole's hand fastened on her wrist. 'You still have questions to answer, elddra,' he hissed.

'Not this night, Syld,' said Tahsin equably. 'You offered Viv en-elddra to my sett, and my sett accepted her. There'll be time for questions on the morrow.'

Viv was surprised when the arsehole released her but as she followed Enesha through a second door into a cool, dark passageway, she was not thinking about Tahsin having bested the arsehole or even about where Enesha took her, but that Tahsin had called the arsehole *Syld*. She had made a deal with the man in the cave to pass on a message to an Eshadi *Syld* and while it galled her to tell the arsehole *anything*, she was bound by the promise.

Enesha was uncommunicative but did exactly as Tahsin requested. She took Viv to a storeroom and collected a neat pile of clothes, some soap, drying cloths, and a comb; showed Viv the washrooms, how warm water was supplied by boilers, and the latrines; then led Viv along another passageway to a small room.

A lamp of patterned glass revealed walls and floors of stone, and a wooden bed, table, two chairs, and clothing chest. The bed was covered with a thick fleece and there was a soft rug under her feet. Viv had not seen such luxury since waking in Ezam.

'You'll be harvesting retsen with me tomorrow and the trees are high,' said Enesha, pausing in the doorway as she left. 'If you've lied about the Waradi *or* about anything else, you won't survive the first day. And that, elddra, is a promise.'

Chapter 20

Viv wedged a chair under the door handle as soon as Enesha had gone and spent the rest of the night pacing. Tahsin seemed friendly and the sett seemed safe, but the arsehole had not brought her here for her benefit. She smiled sourly. She might demand a few answers to her own questions at tomorrow's interrogation and, if Tahsin were there, she might even get them.

The old man's intervention on her behalf had been surprisingly effective, which meant there must be rules about how setts operated, of which she knew nothing. *Hardly surprising, Vivi, considerin' ya know eff-all about anything in this fold.*

She went to the window and cautiously pushed the shutters open. The night air was fragrant and somewhere off in the trees, a bird called. The call echoed her loneliness and her throat tightened. God, how sick she was of being in alien worlds, of being someone's prisoner, of being alone. Thris was out there somewhere, perhaps even on his way back to her, *at this very minute*, but she needed him here *now*.

Shit, she was like a kid whining for a lolly. Wishing for Thris and thinking about him just made it worse. She sighed and her wooden fingers traced the edges of her equally wooden face. 'I *will* heal,' she whispered, as if saying the words aloud lent them power. 'I *will* heal.'

Viv was glad when dawn chased the dark away, as she always was, and to escape her churning thoughts, retraced her steps to the hall where she had eaten last night. She

119

expected the arsehole to be waiting to batter her with questions, but there was only a single man, busy wolfing down bread. Given his height and breadth, Viv guessed he was the lamp-holder from last night.

It took him a while to notice her and then he crammed the last round into his mouth, rose and bowed. 'I am Doran en-Kama-ril,' he mumbled, crumbs spilling down his chin. 'I'm pleased to meet you, Viv en-elddra.'

'I'm pleased to meet you, too,' said Viv, taken aback by his politeness. Only a few lamps had been lit, and she wondered uneasily if the arsehole lurked in the shadows. She jumped as a door opened in the far wall, but the waft of fresh bread told her it led to the kitchen. A thin, dark-haired woman came through carrying a massive tray of the flat, round bread like that Doran had just devoured, and she set it on the table and wiped her floury hands on her apron.

'You must be Viv,' she said. 'I'm Prenya.'

'En-Kama-ril,' added Doran and grinned.

'She's deduced that, you fool,' said Prenya, but Doran continued to grin.

'The elddra's burned her face,' he said, as he reached for more bread.

'And you've lost half your brain,' snapped Prenya. 'You've not set the milk jugs yet, Doran, and for Enda's sake, leave some retsen for the rest of the sett.' She nodded to Viv, picked up the tray, and disappeared back through the door. Doran lumbered after her and soon reappeared with a single jug, which he put on the table, then retrieved a second one.

'Do you want some help?' asked Viv, when he reappeared. At this rate, Doran would be at it all day.

'What?'

120

'Do you want some help with the milk jugs?'

'It's Doran's job to fetch the milk jugs,' he said, 'and guard the sett at night. It's Doran's job to clear the tables after we eat, and to collect and stack the retsen. It's Enesha's job to harvest the retsen.' He nodded, as if to confirm he had got things right, and disappeared back through the door.

Viv loitered nearby while Doran laboriously set the tables with milk jugs, cups and platters, and each time the door opened, Viv heard snatches of conversation and sometimes Prenya's laugh. Doran grinned at Viv when she caught his eye, and she tried to grin back, but her face would not move.

The room had four tables with benches set to each side and, given each bench seated five people, Viv calculated forty people could eat at any given time. She had no idea how big setts usually were, or how many people had been in the room last night, having been in no state to notice anything when the arsehole had dragged her in like some grotesque exhibit. She had no idea why Tahsin had accepted her either. Maybe retsen harvesting was risky or had side effects that killed you, like coal dust that set as hard as concrete in miners' lungs.

The outside door swung open to admit a gust of crisp air and Viv tensed, but it was only Tahsin and Enesha with a net of firewood slung between them. They hauled it through the door to the kitchen and returned a short time later. 'Come and eat, Viv,' said Tahsin, as he and Enesha settled at the table. 'You have a long day ahead of you.'

More people wandered in, some yawning and others scratching their heads, and Viv took a seat opposite him. The hubbub increased and Prenya and a florid-faced man appeared at the kitchen door with trays loaded with bowls of honey, cheese and what looked like yoghurt. The food was passed hand over hand along the tables but waiting for the arsehole to appear made it hard to eat.

'Did you sleep well?' asked Tahsin and Viv's attention jerked back to his furrowed face.

Politeness dictated she say yes but it would not be true. 'I don't sleep very often,' she said apologetically. 'It's nothing to do with the room or bed,' she added quickly. 'They're very nice.'

'I've heard that about the elddra,' said Tahsin as he mixed honey into his yoghurt. 'So, maybe I'll ask whether you rested well instead.' Viv hesitated again and he nodded. 'Who is friend and who is enemy tends to play on the mind in a new sett. Take Enesha here. She could be friend *or* enemy, depending on her mood.'

Enesha did not look up from scooping yoghurt into her mouth. 'Or depending on whether I'm lied to and the sett put at risk,' she said.

Tahsin took a noisy gulp of milk. 'The Syld was concerned about risk too,' he said, 'which is why he left for Esh-accom. He doesn't need to sleep much either,' he added, and started on his bread.

There were four people in the harvesting party: Enesha, Viv, and dark-haired, dark-eyed twin boys who, given their gangliness, Viv guessed were about fourteen. Viv found Fahan and Merhen hard to tell apart but after a while, she noticed Fahan was the more talkative and answered for Merhen even when Enesha addressed Merhen directly. Not that Enesha spoke much, just stomped along, a bulging pack on her back and knives at her belt that looked more like the arsehole's murderous weapons than harvesting knives.

Fahan had taken it upon himself to tell Viv all she needed to know about the Kama-ril, and probably a great deal she did not need to know but she was grateful. Different stands of retsen were harvested in different zadics, he said, and as it was now Cascade, they harvested cloudwise.

Retsen in that sector were the furthest from the sett, on the steepest slopes, and were the tallest, which was why, according to Fahan, it was good Viv had joined the sett. He was happy enough high off the ground but Merhen was not, and Fahan disliked leaving his brother below. Elddra were light, he added, and Viv would have no trouble harvesting to the very tops of the trees.

Enesha's eyes slid sideways in cold appraisal as Fahan spoke, and her thinly veiled threat last night was the reason Viv wore her shirt halter-neck style that morning. It meant if push literally came to shove, she could fly away.

It was close to midday before they reached the retsen stands. The trees soared above their neighbours, their branches thick with green and brown fruit that looked like fibrous avocadoes. Fahan said only the brown were ready for harvesting and there were hundreds of those. Enesha dropped her pack and pulled out bags of knotted cord, a leather pouch of tools, and food that she divvied up. Viv declined her share and the flask that was passed from hand to hand.

'Doran will clean that up,' said Fahan as he eyed her portion. 'He'll be here later to take the bags back.'

The retsen set their lowest branches high off the ground and Viv examined the trees as Enesha hammered in metal climbing spikes. The branches were regular and unless they snapped off like those in the Leferen, should make for an easy climb. She wondered if there were other hazards, such as aggressive birds or animals in the canopy, and hoped that Fahan would have mentioned them.

Enesha called them together to make sure Viv knew how to harvest *properly* but her glare was directed at Fahan and Merhen most of the time, as were her instructions. Knives were *not* to be used due to the trees' height and danger of dropping them; pods were to be snapped off by hand; filled bags were *not* to be released until pickers were absolutely *certain* no one harvested directly beneath them and anyone careless enough to get themselves retsen splinters, would have to wait until Doran or Tahsin had time to get his pliers to them

Viv slung her five bags *that were to be filled before dusk* over her shoulder and followed Enesha up the tree. Enesha climbed quickly, using strength more than skill to haul herself up, and despite seeing better routes, Viv stayed behind her. Sunlight shafted through the leaves and birds like magpies flapped in the branches, but their harsh squawks were nothing like a magpie's yodel.

The boys disappeared beneath the foliage below, but Enesha did not stop until she neared the crown. 'You climb well, elddra,' she said. 'I'm too heavy to go further but you should be able to harvest right to the top. Trust nothing, though. I don't want to explain to Tahsin why I'm a picker short.'

Viv nodded but as she climbed on past, she wondered whether Enesha simply provided herself with an alibi. *I warned her of the dangers, Tahsin. I did my best.* The tree was loaded with pods and Viv slid a bag down her arm and began to pick. The pods snapped off easily, but their fibrous stems were as fine as needles and just as sharp. She sucked out two splinters then acquired several more.

The wind grew and having to balance, *and* pick needed concentration. She worked steadily, tying off each bag and carefully dropping them through the branches, and was on her last bag, and the light fading, when she noticed how quiet it was. And then, right on cue, Enesha climbed up through the leaves and propped herself between Viv and the trunk.

'Time to answer some questions, elddra,' she said and unsheathed her knife. Viv tied off the last bag and let it go, keeping her gaze on it as she slipped open her jacket buttons. 'I've sent the boys back with Doran,' said Enesha. 'It's up to you whether you come back as well.'

'I thought it was up to Tahsin,' said Viv, more calmly than she felt.

Enesha shrugged. 'Tahsin trusts too easily but I won't risk this sett suffering the same fate as Esh-embrin.'

'What is it you want to know?'

'The Syld who brought you here is known as Mad At, not because he's a fool or a liar, but because he knows no fear. He said you had a Waradi lein-tryst and I'm inclined to believe him.'

'He thinks that because I was with a Waradi and wore a Waradi tryst-bracelet.'

Enesha's face hardened. 'A pretty reasonable conclusion, wouldn't you say?'

'But a wrong one. I took the bracelet from the Lefer. It was being used to make them fight so men could bet on the outcome. I didn't know what it was. It was pretty, and I kept it.'

Enesha gave a bark of laughter. 'Your lies amuse me, elddra. Add to my enjoyment by concocting an equally entertaining tale about why you were with the Waradi.'

Viv opened her mouth, but the words would not come. *He chased me and caught me and raped me.* Why could she not say it? She groped for the absent feather at her neck and Enesha paled. 'You have no amé!'

'It was destroyed.' Viv was tempted to say how but lessening the respect Sylds seemed to enjoy might jeopardise Poss's safety

'Why were you with the Waradi?' repeated Enesha, but her voice was subdued now, as if she had lost her appetite for the answer.

'I was like the bracelet,' said Viv bitterly. 'He thought I was pretty and he took me.' The question of rape hung between them, unasked and unanswered. 'What else do you want to know?'

'Nothing,' said Enesha and sheathed her knife. 'It's time we got back. Prenya hates people being late for her cooking.'

Chapter 21

The days fell into the type of routine Viv had last experienced in jail. Life with Jimmy Wright and the gangs had been chaotic, and her transits with Thris had hardly gone to plan, so the sett's predictability eased the knot in her stomach. She joined the early risers for breakfast and ate retsen dipped in honey, not because she was hungry, but because Doran said the sett ate together, and she was part of the sett.

But no matter how early she rose, Doran beat her to the hall to demolish the first rounds of retsen and laboriously set the tables. Viv gave up offering to help him and to help Enesha and Tahsin who delivered the firewood each morning. Jobs were assigned, Enesha told her, and Viv had hers. Tahsin had not disputed Enesha's claim, in fact, Viv had never seen him dispute with anyone over anything except the arsehole.

Enesha asked Viv no more questions and while she was no longer hostile, now was she friendly. She led Viv, Fahan and Merhen out each day and told them the trees to be harvested, the number of bags to be filled, and when it was time to turn for home. She spoke only to deliver instructions or to criticise the twins on their work output and Doran on his infinite capacity to eat.

Enesha was taciturn by nature but Fahan chatted to Viv all the way to the retsen stands and all the way back. Merhen said nothing but she caught his gaze on her more than once. She enjoyed her time high in the retsens where she harvested alone but it was not just the birds and dappled sunlight that lifted her spirits; there was an itch in her hands and face that surely meant she healed.

Viv had been in the sett over a week when their group was joined by two new pickers, younger men called Cazir and Jered. She wondered why Tahsin had enlarged their team and it was only when Jered took up position next to Enesha, and Cazir brought up the rear, that she suspected they were guards.

Jered and Enesha's conversation was too low for Viv to hear but Fahan's chatter suggested he was not aware of any threat and she glanced back at Cazir. He wore several knives at his belt, which was not unusual, for Enesha carried them too, but Cazir's hand rested on the haft of one and his gaze searched their surroundings.

Enesha gave the men only a couple of bags to fill and both chose to harvest in Viv's tree. Their presence put her even more on edge, and she was distracted enough to collect several painful splinters before she filled her bags and dropped them to the forest floor.

As usual it was dusk before they started back and Viv so tense she scarcely noticed when Fahan joined Cazir at the back, and shy Merhen moved up to walk beside her. If Jered and Cazir *were* guards, then something must have happened. It might be that fighting had broken out nearby but if so, she would have heard about it as they took their meals in the hall or at least noticed some worried looks. Everything in the sett seemed normal and she had a horrible feeling Cazir and Jered's presence had something to do with her.

'How did you burn your face?' asked Merhen.

'What?' asked Viv, jerked from her thoughts.

'Your face. How did you burn it?'

'She's been in the Grey Fire,' said Fahan, coming level.

'Only the Stonash travel the Grey Fire,' said Merhen, clearly puzzled and when Viv still said nothing, murmured, 'I bet you were pretty before.'

Enesha was ahead but she rounded on him furiously. 'Pretty? Why must a woman be pretty? To please you or some other stone-hearted man? Who are you to judge if a woman is pretty?'

Merhen's face was scarlet as he stuttered an apology and for once Fahan did not defend him but walked with his eyes on the ground. 'I know you didn't mean any harm, Merhen,' said Viv, hating to see him upset. 'Elddra heal from most injuries. Maybe one day you'll see me as I was before.'

Viv spent a long time in the washrooms that night as the itch in her hands and face suddenly escalated. 'Worse than a thousand bloody mozzie bites,' she mumbled, as she scratched at her scalp, then gasped as chunks of leathery skin came away. She hardly dared breathe as she used her comb to rid herself of the mess and piled it high on the bench. 'I have the worst case of dandruff in the entire Rynth,' she muttered and giggled in delight.

If only the washroom had a mirror! Her face was still rigid but as she flexed her hands, the hard skin peeled away like gloves to reveal the perfect skin beneath. Viv sagged against the wall in relief. The burns to her face were no worse but the skin remained stiff and unmoving, and she scrunched her shed skin into a ball, stuffed it in her pocket, and hastened back to her room then on an impulse, knocked on Enesha's door. 'Who is it?' came Enesha's gruff voice.

'It's Viv. Do you have a mirror?'

'A mirror?'

There were no sounds of footsteps on the other side and Viv was forced to speak to the wood. 'A looking-glass,' she said, wondering if they were called something else here.

'I know what a mirror is,' snapped Enesha. 'Do you think I have the trade of a Syld? If you want a mirror, ask your friend Mad At.'

Viv went to her room and jammed the chair under the handle. The hardened skin on her face remained unmoving but she worked her shaking fingers around her hairline, seeking some sort of edge, and screwed her face up and down in exaggerated expressions. And then, in one exquisite moment, the whole lot came away, to leave her holding a mask of her own face.

Viv staggered under an onslaught of emotions. Relief at having escaped disfigurement, fury at what the arsehole had inflicted, triumph at having beaten him, all mixed with the sobering understanding of what it was like to be judged ugly in the world. Tahsin had accepted her grotesque appearance, as he had accepted the slow-witted Doran, and the mannish Enesha, and she felt a surge of gratitude for the old sett leader.

She put the ball of shed skin on the table but set the mask on the chest next to the urrut collar and leash. They were trophies that marked her victories over the arsehole, and if he had not stolen the tryst-bracelet, she would have lined that up too.

Her healing meant she no longer had any reason to delay in the fold, but she must farewell Poss first. Then she would return to the rift in the Leferen if she had to, or to the one in the cave where she had found Poss, and she would fly, using speed and darkness, to keep herself safe.

130

The zadic ignited beyond the window and on an impulse, Viv undressed, unbedded her wings, and thrust the shutters wide. Her wings sparked silver in the starry brilliance, and she beat them, intoxicated by their beauty. The room filled with her potent scent and then a twig cracked, and she threw herself into the wall's deep shadow. A bird flapped away and there was a furtive step, then another heavier one and the sound of humming. It was Doran making his nightly rounds and her breath emptied. She had been a fool to risk discovery, she conceded, as she fastened the shutters and dressed.

A feather glimmered on the floor and she tucked it away in her pocket. She would give it to Poss for her collection and to remember her by, but Viv needed nothing to remember Poss by; the little girl engraved on her heart.

The shed skin sat in a misshapen ball on the table and Viv grimaced. She could hardly toss it in with the food scraps and the mild nights meant only the kitchen fire remained alight. The mask looked repugnant too, more like a dead animal than any trophy and would tell pursuers, like the Waradi rapist, she had been here, so she rolled it up with the rest of the skin and made her way stealthily to the hall.

The tables were deserted but a single lamp burned, and she crept past it to the door that led to the kitchen and eased it open, nonplussed to find another passageway. She stole down it, hoping to God the door at the end *was* the kitchen, and hissed in relief when it was.

Bowls gleamed in the fire's glow and Viv slid between the scrubbed benches and dropped the dead skin onto the coals. There was a hiss as the flames flared and the ball of skin shrivelled, and then it was gone. She remained where she was, her gaze on the coals, aware that more than her skin had burned away, and then there was a shout.

Viv's heart jolted and she crouched instinctively and searched the darkness then there was a second shout and the thump of running feet. No one burst into the kitchen and she crept back along the passageway nerves stretched to breaking point. If she had broken some sort of rule, it would be best to high tail it back to her room but as she slid into the hall, she was seized and slammed back against the wall.

A lamp was thrust in her face, blinding her, and there was a tingling hiatus. 'A stranger and yet not a stranger,' sounded Tahsin's voice. 'It's time we talked.'

Chapter 22

Viv sat at the table at the far end of the hall, glad it was Tahsin who had caught her, and not someone else. He stood near the kitchen door in conversation with Doran, Cazir and Jered, and all four stared in her direction. Then the group broke and Tahsin came back, set the lamp on the table, and sat opposite. 'Why were you in the kitchen?' he asked directly.

'The dead skin came off my face and hands and I went there to burn it.'

'Why not wait until morning and dispose of it in the refuse?'

'It … didn't look nice. Burning was cleaner.'

'Why not wait until morning?' he pursued.

'I was going to leave tonight.'

'To go where?'

'Esh-accom.'

'Elddra avoid settlements, especially large ones. Why Esh-accom?'

'I need to farewell someone.'

'The Syld's daughter you cared for?' Viv blinked in surprise. 'Cazir and Jered have lately returned from there. They say the streets are abuzz with the miraculous recovery of Ataghan en-Scinta-ril's daughter, and that the child owes her life to an elddra. The elddra speak of it too but less openly. Elddra are known to each other but this elddra is known to no one.'

Viv struggled to hold Tahsin's gaze. Even had she been capable of lying, she would not have lied to this man but there were so much she could not tell him. The silence stretched and Tahsin pulled a small wooden box from his pocket and set it on the table. 'Do you know what this is?' he asked. Viv shook her head. 'It's called Enda's Aim.'

He removed the top and emptied coloured glass balls into his hand, then turned the box over to reveal a series of lines and holes on its base. 'The challenge is to create a pattern with the balls while avoiding the lines. Succeed and you're closer to Enda's aim, fail and you're closer to Soaich's.

'Enda's Aim is a type of puzzle,' he said, tipping the balls back into the box and slipping it into his pocket. Viv braced for more questions, but the door opened and Tahsin ordered her to wait. Viv did not turn to see who had entered but the drift of light told her dawn was close and that others would soon arrive to breakfast. She ran her fingers over the new skin of her face. The mask of burned skin had hidden her strangeness and without it, she felt almost naked. Maybe she should have accepted the arsehole's offer of a piece of cloth after all!

Tahsin returned juggling plates of retsen, a jar of honey, and two cups of water. 'Eat,' he said. Viv broke the retsen, dipped it in the honey, and ate. 'Many of my sett were born elsewhere,' said Tahsin as he started on his own food. 'Enesha arrived almost five zadicans ago. Her love is for women, not men. Doran's been part of the sett for two zadicans. He carries his strength in his hands and heart, not in his head. Prenya and Borish arrived together. Borish is sterile but Prenya won't take another lover and so denied her sett the gift of children.

'Fahan and Merhen were only ten zadicans when they arrived half starved. Some vals see twins as a curse. They believe the second child steals the strength of the first child and if the second child dies, the strength will be restored.

Merhen's shyness made him vulnerable but twins are closer than lein, and Fahan brought his brother here.

'Enesha has never confided in me and nor have the others. Like Enda's Aim, they were puzzles, but Tahsin en-Kama-ril likes puzzles.' He took a swig of water and wiped the wetness from his chin. 'One night, the powerful Syld Ataghan en-Scinta-ril arrives at Tahsin's sett with Viv en-elddra. Both bear the burns of the Grey Fire, but the elddra's burns are many times worse. The Syld's antagonism for the elddra is strong yet it is a shadow of her hatred for him. The Syld later tells Tahsin en-Kama-ril the elddra wore a Waradi tryst-bracelet and kept company with the Waradi leader.'

'I did have a bracelet,' admitted Viv and recounted how she came by it.

'And the Waradi leader?'

'He caught me,' she muttered as the familiar churn started in her stomach.

'The elddra has a small urrut collar and leash in her room,' said Tahsin. 'Both have been cut.'

'As Enesha's searched my room, maybe she can solve the puzzle,' said Viv sourly.

'Tahsin's the sett's puzzle-solver,' he said equably. 'Enesha doesn't have the patience.' He took another gulp of water. 'Tahsin thinks the solution to the puzzle is this: the Syld believes Viv en-elddra is the Waradi leader's lein-tryst but is stopped from killing her by his lein, who is known to be a very different sort of man. But the Syld remains determined to destroy her and tethers her to a Stonash urrut-trade knowing the Grey Fire will complete the task. Then he learns his daughter lives because of the elddra. The debt requires he retrieve her, but his suspicion remains, so he brings her to Tahsin en-Kama-ril's sett, far enough from Esh-accom and his own val to forget she ever existed.'

'Tahsin is a good puzzle-solver,' said Viv thickly.

'Tahsin has had lots of practice but he has solved only half of this puzzle. The other half is *who* Viv en-elddra is, or perhaps *what* Viv en-elddra is.' Viv hugged herself but could think of nothing to say. 'Tahsin likes solving puzzles, not hurting people,' he added softly, but Viv kept her gaze on the table.

'There was a stranger in the sett last night,' he said abruptly. 'He, or others, have been seen by Doran during Enesha's harvests, and yet no other harvesters have seen strangers. Even before the fighting, Tahsin en-Kama-ril's sett has never turned away the hungry, but this stranger shows no courtesy. He does not knock at our door but seeks entry through your window. He follows your harvesting party and seeks out your room. Can you help solve the puzzle for Tahsin, Viv en-elddra?'

The rapist's face flashed before her eyes and Viv clamped her hand over her mouth and dashed from the hall, reaching the chill air outside before the water, retsen and honey, emptied onto the grass. Her stomach continued to heave, and it was Enesha, not Tahsin, who gave her a damp cloth to wipe her mouth.

'I'll take you to your room,' said Enesha, and hauled her up, but when she lowered Viv onto a bed, it was in a different room entirely. 'Not as nice a view,' said Enesha, pushing the shutters wide, 'but harder to get to for uninvited guests.' The room looked onto the central courtyard, which meant it was in the innermost part of the sett, but if the intruder *were* the Waradi rapist, navigating a few passageways and killing a few people along the way was not going to deter him.

Enesha plonked onto a chair and surveyed her with arms crossed. 'You're in the men's part of the sett,' she said. 'Cazir's room is to your left and Jered's to your right. You'll be the envy of every woman here once Fire Zadic starts, or almost every woman,' she added dryly.

Viv swallowed several times. 'Did he hurt anyone?' she croaked.

'Who?'

'The man who tried to break in.'

'Doran's got a few stitches in his arm, but he was always as slow as an urrut.'

'He'll come back, and more people will get hurt. I should leave.'

'You think it's the Waradi, don't you?'

'Yes.'

'It's one of the reasons elddra are disliked,' she said, and Viv looked at her blankly. 'During rut, maragh sows give off a scent that boars can't resist. They've been known to starve to death waiting for sows to come back.' Enesha shrugged.' It's said that once a man tastes elddra scent, he'll go nowhere else. Meanwhile, Valen women wait in line and setts are denied children.'

Enesha's voice was heavy with sarcasm but Viv's dread grew. The Waradi had only given her up when cornered by the arsehole. *I own you, lein-tryst, remember that.* Viv's stomach heaved, and she sucked in more air.

'Are you going to be sick again?' asked Enesha.

'No.'

Enesha picked up the urrut collar and turned it over in her hands. 'Of course, everything I've said could be generated by good old-fashioned jealousy. With a face like yours, you've no need to scent mark, not that it's had any amorous effect on Mad At.' She tossed the urrut collar onto the chest and went to the door. 'We're not harvesting today, Tahsin says we deserve a rest, but don't go off anywhere without asking him. It's his sett and you need his permission to leave, elddra or not.'

Sehereden rode out of Esh-accom at dusk and struck cloudwise, Fara seeming as happy as him to be quit of the settlement. Fariye had been happy too, and excited to go back to Brithergen's compound, given her belief Sehereden's departure hastened the return of her da and lein.

Fara stretched out in a gallop but Sehereden instructed him to slow when the dark thickened and to quicken again when the Cascade Zadic doused the val with silver. If Ataghan *were* to return, he would come starwise in the next few days, and Sehereden wanted to aid the final part of his lein's journey.

He stopped only to allow Fara to drink from rills and as the night grew old, and a mist rolled in, turned up the val's side, and reached the ridge top as the new sun broke the crests. Then he slid from Fara's back and let the stallion graze as he settled on a tor. The mist glittered below him like a golden sea, but his thoughts turned to Astraal's sacred lake and those who had seeded the elddra.

It was hard to be part Valen and part Angellus or rather, part *Astraali*, if Mareva-en-Thinda-ril was to be believed, and he wondered why Viv had left the sacred city's safety. The elddra in Esh-accom wanted . . . Fara's head came up and Sehereden crouched and drew his knife. *Who*? he asked, but the stallion sent no images, intent on the val below.

138

Then Fara whickered and Sehereden's heart leapt. The val might be full of mist but Fara's reaction told him it was Ataghan and Sehereden offered up thanks to Enda, vaulted back on the stallion, and rode down to meet his lein.

Their return to Esh-accom was slowed by Fara carrying two, but Sehereden soon learned Viv was at Tahsin en-Kama-ril's sett. She had survived the Grey Fire but not unscathed, and was *as the Stonash*, his lein told him briefly.

'She might still recover,' said Sehereden. 'Elddra are known for their healing powers.'

'Her *healing powers* kept her alive, lein, but they will do no more,' said Ataghan. 'She'll make her home with others whose strangeness excludes them from normal setts.'

He had then outlined his strategies to rid the Eshavale of remnant Ascadi and Waradi fighters, and afterwards, how his sett was to be rebuilt, but Sehereden's thoughts remained on Viv. She had been condemned to the most terrible of futures and while he could not undo what had been done, nor could he walk away.

He doubted Anfarena's interest would wane either. He needed to see Viv one last time if only to express his regret. He remained haunted by his last sight of her and whatever the nature of their next parting, it had to be better than that.

Chapter 23

Thris was relieved to hear no yowls of beastmen in the next fold, in fact, it looked like the fold where he, Ky and Viv had been attacked by the long arm caste. The sky was blue, there was a single sun, and the land had mountains, trees and birdsong. But if it were the same fold, he was in a different sector.

He stowed his shirt and jacket in his pack and reconnoitred. The ground had been burned, but it was not recent; green plant caste having intruded into the black, and beyond the ruined buildings, there was a neat stack of burned human caste bones, a practice he had observed in other human caste folds.

He detoured around the bones and stopped. There was rift and it held Viv's print, but rifts did not reveal whether the traveller had entered or exited. This eyed his surroundings thoughtfully. Given their similarity to Moonsun, *if* Viv had exited here, she might have stayed.

He turned up slope, keeping a careful eye on his surroundings. The ruined buildings and dead human caste were likely the result of fighting and such folds were perilous. If Viv were here, he would transit her out immediately *assuming* her mother was not here too. Given his pledge to keep Viv safe, it was yet another conundrum he faced, but first he must find her.

He was a long way up the slope when he came across a cave filled with dried human caste waste. Human caste had strict protocols for disposing of their bodily excesses and he had never known them to use caves. The cave also held a rift and while he sensed Viv's resonance in the cave, it was not in the rift, which confirmed his guess she had stayed.

He went on and by the time he reached the top of the ridge, the sky's blue had been replaced with a soft orange. The colour woke an intense longing for Ezam's symmetry but as he stared down, the fold's criss-crossed valleys mirrored the discord of its human caste inhabitants instead, and he stared up towards the crest.

Something gleamed beyond the next ridge and while he decided it was a strip of cloud, caught by the last of the sun's rays, the sight resonated deep in his angelic being. He did not rouse until the dark cycle and then, disturbed by his loss of awareness, he secured his pack to his waist and took to the air.

Dark valleys unfolded beneath him, aglint with the rush of water, but the stars were dim, and he descended for a better view and discovered the fold was far from chaotic. Huge ridges fanned out from a central peak like the petals of a mighty glis bloom, to enclose smaller ridges and valleys that ran in parallel. Smudges of gold and drifts of smoke heralded human caste settlements and then the sky erupted with a brilliance that doused him in starlight. A constellation rippled across the heavens like a river of burning water and he hovered entranced.

It illuminated a pale band of grasslands directly below him, with a boundary as precise as the Dendrinai's, but as he pondered what else the fold might share with Ezam, dark shapes erupted from the trees. For a moment, he thought they were angels, then the starlight revealed their webbed wings, and the night filled with their stench.

Thris powered skyward but the creatures were fast, and he dived instead. The attackers' momentum carried them past but as he swept along the treetops, one burst through the canopy and cannoned into him. Its claws raked his side and the shock sent Thris smashing along the treetops before he managed to right himself, gain height, and fly on. Blood gushed from the gash with every wingbeat and, as the trees gave way to the grasslands, he came to ground.

The creatures had not followed but he was horribly exposed, and he broke into a staggering run and managed to get airborne again. He could barely fly and spread his wings to glide, knowing he must find shelter to rest and heal, and then the ground disappeared and there was a yawning chasm, the fume of falling water, and its roar as it rushed along the valley floor.

Thris's strength failed and he vaned his wings back in a desperate attempt to slow his descent, clipped the top of a tree and spun sideways into another. Its branches broke his fall as he crashed through them to where its gnarled roots thrust from the forest floor. Thris crawled in amongst them and managed to bed his wings before utter blackness took him.

Thris knew nothing of the lamp that bobbed through the trees, or of the men with their ropes and clubs. Nor did he witness their astonishment. 'That's no sap-sucker,' the first man whispered as he held the lamp high.

'Nor a man to survive such a fall, Worach,' the other replied.

''E's not survived it yet,' said Worach. ''E's bleedin' like a rill in flood.'

'They'll be cloth in his bag. Bind him up. He's no use to us dead. We'll take him back and see what the mornin' shows.'

'I'd rather eat 'im,' grumbled Worach.

The other man laughed. 'A sap-sucker'll give you a few meals but I'm guessin' that with the festivities comin' up, this *thing* will give us many.' He smiled down at Thris's perfect face. 'Even the elddra will part with their precious traders to see a livin', breathin' Angellus.'

'An Angellus, Yerden? Where's 'is wings?'

'You saw him fly and you saw him come down. He's put them away, that's all. With the right encouragement, I'm sure he'll show them again. Are you done there yet? Bind his hands and feet while you're at it. We don't want him wakin' up while we're on the way back.'

Worach did as he was bid, and then he took Thris's shoulders and Yerden his feet, and they hauled him out of the trees into the Zadic's fading light. ''E's not very heavy,' said Worach, in surprise, as they started back.

'The Angellus are known for that too,' said Yerden.

Ash circled the Green Helixai, in no hurry to land. Ledges were scarce, unlike the other Helixai, but that was not the only reason he delayed. He had been here eons ago, with Thris and Ky when new to Ezam, and he remembered it as green stone, but what confronted him now was fallen timber, rampant vines, and the stench of decay.

He finally found a patch of clear ground and landed, and not knowing what else to do, clambered into the tangle. The Blue Helixai had granted him blissful dream-like trances, and the White an ethereal meditative beauty, but he feared the Green had more in common with the Red, whose flames had forced him deep into its dark heart.

He struggled onwards, hoping to find a cavern like those that pocked the other Helixai, but found more tangled growth instead. The vines tore feathers from his wings, but he kept them unbedded in case he must fly.

Prime-archaes Mirek and Serith believed he replicated Senquar-archae's route to transcendence, but no one knew whether Senquar-archae *had* transcended. He might have been marooned or destroyed in an alien fold. Ash stared around uneasily. Glis shed leaves but not twigs or branches and he was horrified by the notion that glis could topple The Dendrinai's decay was infinitesimally slow, rendering it curiously unchanging, but here the rot unwove the Helixai before his very eyes.

Even the ground was unstable. It flexed under his feet or was saturated with a foul ooze that bubbled and hissed, and he was soon besmirched with putrid juices. He struggled on, searching for the green stone he remembered, and finding only rank growth. He was surrounded by hundreds of shades of green and he peered up, desperate for a glimpse of Ezam's peach sky, missed his footing and fell. Even his wings were befouled now, and he struggled upright and slumped onto a nearby log. At least the sludge hid the undeserved white plumage in his wings!

Archae Mirek might be convinced the Blue, White and Red Helixai had granted Ash the white of ascension for a reason, but Ash had never deciphered what it was and could make no sense of his present predicament either. The Host were right to ignore the Helixai, he concluded morosely, and yet Archae Mirek believed them to be important, as did Archae Serith, even before the Archae had discovered Senquar-archae's words.

Light is the lure and light the trap; light the maze and light the map. The red, the blue, and the white won't show, what mantise, scarab and sumi know.

What could Ezam's animal caste possibly know that lay hidden in the Blue's resonant music? In the Red's cleansing fire? In the White's deep illumination? What had the other blue angel discovered here that was so important that Prime Archaes Mirek and Serith believed *he* must discover it too? And important to whom? Just him? Or to the entire Host?

He went on, wiping ineffectually at the slime that covered him. Maybe what mantise, scarab and sumi *knew* was that the Green Helixai seethed with more questions than answers. Maybe . . . The tangle beneath his feet moved and then gave way, and he was plunged into the Helixai's fetid darkness.

Chapter 24

Sehereden set camp high in the vals, cheered by knowing he would be in the Kama-ril on the morrow. His meeting with Viv would not be easy but he remained convinced it was necessary, despite his lein's reaction. Ataghan had not hidden his anger at Sehereden's plans and while leins authority over each other flowed from love, their leinship was complicated by Ataghan being Syld, and Sehereden serving in his band.

Fire Zadic's approach prompted the temporary dissolution of bands to allow men to train for the tournaments, which meant that for the present, Ataghan could not order Sehereden, or any other band member, to do anything.

But Sehereden was still troubled by his lein's displeasure as he set his maark. Ataghan had refused to discuss Viv's predicament beyond suggesting Sehereden's interest stemmed from lust. *Don't waste your time chasing elddra, Sehereden. Hone your skills with me and you'll have your pick of many blue-eyed women come the festivities.* Sehereden did not believe his lein's summation was correct but he supposed he would not know for sure until he saw Viv again.

Viv dropped the last bag of retsen pods through the branches and slowly swung herself down, in no rush to join those on the ground. Cazir and Jered had made no effort to hide their interest since she had shed her rucked mask of a face and even Fahan's boyish admiration made her uncomfortable.

At least Doran and Enesha's attitudes had not changed: the former still oblivious and the latter still indifferent. Viv had taken to walking at Enesha's shoulder which Enesha ignored, and that suited Viv. She much preferred a woman who spurned her company, to the men who did not.

It was almost a week since the attempted break in and since Viv had learned how elddra scent was rumoured to trap men, and she wondered if it were the reason for the Waradi's dogged pursuit of her. Thris's sweetness had certainly intensified their love making, she recalled uneasily.

Jered and Cazir's muscularity suggested they were good fighters, but Viv scanned the darkening trees as they walked, the Waradi never far from her thoughts. She should have left by now but had no idea where Esh-accom was in relation to Tahsin's sett. It sounded like a decent-sized settlement, and its lamps should be visible from above, but not wanting to risk herself in the air was not the only reason she delayed. Staying in one place made it easier for Thris to find her.

'We've got a visitor,' said Enesha, as they neared the sett, 'or you have. Looks like the quality of horse a Syld would ride.'

Viv stopped so suddenly Cazir all but cannoned into her and he took the opportunity to put his hands lightly on her waist, as if to steady himself. Viv barely noticed, her attention on the stallion in the sett's yards. It stared directly at her. 'Now the Syld knows you're here too,' added Enesha, enjoying Viv's discomfort.

'But it's the wrong colour,' blurted Viv. The arsehole and his cronies had ridden horses with *black* manes and tails, yet this horse had a *silver* mane and tail.

147

'I've no idea what black hole of a val your mother raised you in,' broke in Enesha's scathing voice, 'but even you should know the colour of Eshadi horses!'

She stomped off to the hall, but Viv went to her room and wedged a chair under the handle. Poss had told her Eshadi horses were charcoal with silver manes and tails and had suggested a mental link between Eshadi horses and their owners, that Enesha had just confirmed, so swapping horses seemed unlikely.

None of it made sense but it no longer mattered. She could not have had a clearer wake-up call to quit the sett than the arsehole's return. The advantage of owning nothing was that it took no time to pack, she concluded acidly, as she thrust the urrut collar and leash into her pocket, and followed it more gently with the feather for Poss. And as the arsehole was *here*, he was in no position to prevent her visiting his daughter in Esh-accom.

Viv was halfway down the passageway before she remembered Enesha's strictures about leaving without Tahsin's permission, but it was his kindness that stopped her from slinking off. He had given a despised and disfigured elddra a place in his sett *and* he had protected her since. She owed him a formal thank you, if nothing else.

She returned to her room and settled on the bed. She would wait until the sett had quieted and visit him at his room. There were rules around men visiting the women's rooms, but Viv did not think the reverse were true and she grinned as she imagined Tahsin's reaction. No doubt he would tell her if she were wrong.

Sehereden was disappointed when Viv did not appear to eat with the rest of her harvesting party. Tahsin introduced them but only Enesha, who he had first mistaken for a man, settled at his table. 'She lost her appetite when I mistook your horse for your lein's,' she said cheerfully. 'Not that she's got much of an appetite. The sett certainly got the better end of the deal when she joined us. Works all day without complaint, on the highest retsens where even our bravest men fear to tread, and barely eats at all, let alone enough to balance her keep, eh Tahsin?' Tahsin nodded and continued his conversation with the man seated behind him.

Enesha more than made up for Viv's lack of appetite, concluded Sehereden, as he watched her work her way through a stack of retsen. The rest of the harvesting party consisted of the man-mountain Doran, whose brain did not match his brawn; the twins Merhen and Fahan, who still dreamed of bedding their first woman; and Jered and Cazir, clearly veterans of more than one tournament. They watched him in the measuring way common as Fire Zadic approached, and he watched them.

'Not our best pickers,' said Enesha, following his gaze, 'but handy with knives. Tahsin's told you the elddra brought trouble with her?'

'He said there had been strangers about, at least one of whom lacked the usual courtesies.'

'The one who tried to break into Viv's room certainly did,' said Enesha, starting on her second bowl of gorash.

Sehereden lowered his voice. 'My lein believes she's trysted to the Waradi leader. Do you think it's him?'

'Viv's denied being trysted to anyone and most of the sett believe elddra don't lie.'

'And you? What do you believe?'

149

'That elddra are as capable of lying as the rest of us.' Enesha licked the last of the gorash from her spoon, then brought her hard eyes to his. 'But mention the man's name and she vomits. That's a hard thing to pull off as deception, Ataghan's lein. Much harder than lying.'

Viv waited until the zadic had come and gone before she made her way stealthily along the passageway but there was no answer to her furtive knock on Tahsin's door and she chewed her lip as she considered whether he slept. She did not want to wake the men who slept nearby by knocking louder and had decided to leave without a formal farewell when she heard voices from the hall.

Most of the sett had gone to their beds but Tahsin was at the far table in conversation with Doran. The lamp at their table had burned low and she was halfway across the hall before she realised a third person sat with them in the shadows. Tahsin finished whatever he said to Doran, and Doran lumbered past, but Viv remained frozen in the middle of the floor.

'Are you going to stay there all night or join us?' called Tahsin.

Viv forced her limbs into action and heard a sharp intake of breath as she stepped into the lamplight. The other man's shock was matched by Viv's. It was not the arsehole after all but his lein and she was struck afresh by his likeness to Rim *and* then by the memory of his willingness to have her hauled away to her death.

'You know Sehereden en-Scinta-ril, I believe,' said Tahsin.

'Yes,' said Viv, keeping her gaze on Tahsin.

'There's something you want to speak to me about?' prompted Tahsin.

'Yes,' said Viv again, and hesitated, not wanting the arsehole's lein to witness her farewell to the man who had shown her kindness.

The silence stretched and Sehereden rose but Tahsin waved him back. 'Stay Sehereden, if you would. This might concern you.'

Viv licked her lips. *Get on with it, Vivi*, Rim's contemptuous voice intruded. 'I'm leaving tonight and Enesha said I should ask your permission.' Shit, that was not what she had intended to say!

'Those of my sett come and go as they wish, Viv. It's a courtesy to tell me you'll be away for a time, that's all. It helps me plan the work teams and, in your case, let's me know you've come to no harm.'

'I wanted to say thank you for letting me stay *and* for making me welcome,' she said thickly. Viv had forgotten the arsehole's lein now as she thought only of Tahsin's generosity.

'You're a member of Tahsin's sett now. You can be absent for zadicans and that won't change. Even if the pyre's taken me, the sett will be here, and so will your place.'

Viv's throat tightened, and it was Tahsin who broke the silence. 'You're going to Esh-accom?' Viv nodded. 'Sehereden en-Scinta-ril's told me what you did for his lein's daughter. There's love between you?'

'Yes.'

'Something Sehereden confirms. The little girl pines for her lein,' said Tahsin, with a smile. 'That's why I ask that you accept Sehereden's offer of an escort.'

'No!'

'We both know the danger waiting for you beyond this sett,' said Tahsin quietly.

'*He* won't catch me a second time,' said Viv wildly.

'Why not?'

The question was simple but hard to answer. 'I had to draw them away from Poss last time but now I only have myself to worry about,' she muttered.

'I understand why you don't want my company,' said Sehereden, entering the conversation for the first time, 'but you and I have one thing in common: we both love my lein's daughter and I won't go back to Esh-accom and tell her I abandoned you to a dangerous journey on your own.'

'Then don't tell her!' said Viv, rounding on him. 'You can add it to all the other things you won't tell her like your lein sending me into the ice-fire!'

'You're correct in that I won't tell her anything that undermines her trust in her father.'

'*Choose*-father,' sneered Viv but it was a moot point. Children in this fold were cherished, biological or not, and it galled Viv she could not tell Poss what her father had done for the same reason. 'I'm leaving now,' she said but knew she had lost the argument.

'Fara awaits,' said Sehereden with a bow. Viv glanced back to Tahsin and quelled an impulse to hug him. It was hard to remember a time when a man's arms had not delivered violence along with any tenderness.

'A fair journey to you, Viv,' said Tahsin with a nod. 'And a fair journey to you also, Sehereden en-Scinta-ril. And remember that you guard not only a member of Tahsin en-Kama-ril's sett, but an elddra, and elddra aren't like those Enda might gift you at Fire Zadic.'

Viv sensed Tahsin had delivered some sort of warning, but the arsehole's lein simply bowed, thanked Tahsin for his welcome and hospitality, and followed her out.

Chapter 25

Viv waited in the chill night air while Sehereden brought his forehead to his horse's and murmured something too low for Viv to hear. She already regretted her decision to journey with him. If she had held out, she could have been halfway to Esh-accom by now.

Wood smoke blossomed from the chimney behind her, and she guessed Borish had replenished the kitchen's fire. Soon Prenya would join him to start the day's baking and Doran would come in from his rounds and wolf-down the first batch of retsen. Her throat tightened as she realised that Tahsin was the first person in her life to gift her a home.

Sehereden vaulted onto his horse and secured his pack to a strap about the horse's neck. It was the only harness he used, unlike the Waradi. 'Would you like to ride in front or behind?' he asked as he extended his hand.

'I'm walking.'

'Esh-accom is a three-day ride, *if* all goes well, and a seven-day walk, *if* all goes well. If you walk, I'll have to walk too, and my capacity to ensure your safety will be compromised.'

'I never asked you to *ensure my safety*.'

'No, your sett leader did. But even if he hadn't, I'd do it for Fariye's sake. She's lost enough loved ones, without losing you.'

Sehereden had just bested her again and Viv ground her teeth. Being beaten by words was no more enjoyable than being beaten by fists, but she sourly acknowledged it was less painful. 'I'll ride behind,' she muttered.

'Have you ridden before?' he asked, as he hefted her on.

'Not since I was a child.'

'How long ago was that?'

'A while.'

'I can ask Fara to go faster if you're an experienced rider.'

'Tell him to go at a snail's pace.'

'A *snail*?'

'Tell him to go slow.' They set off and Viv screwed her head around for one last look at the sett knowing she would never see it again.

'It's good you have a sett to return to,' said Sehereden. 'Ataghan's sett was burned.'

'I know. We went there.'

'So Fariye said. Is there nothing left?'

'Just the store. Poss showed me.'

'Why do you call her Poss?'

'It's a nickname. She didn't tell me her real name until we became lein, and that was just before . . . we were separated.' Viv took several deep breaths to settle her stomach. 'Did she reach Esh-accom on her own?'

'She was found within sight of the walls.'

'And she's happy now? There are children to play with there, and adults who love her?'

'Of course, but she hasn't forgotten her lein.' He smiled back at her. '*When will Viv come? When will Viv come?* She gives us no peace.'

Viv looked away. 'She'll forget about me soon enough.'

'Leins don't forget each other.'

'I'm going to Esh-accom to say goodbye and then I'm leaving.'

'That makes no difference. Leins are one until death, and perhaps after, although only Enda knows that.' Sehereden paused. 'If you didn't want a permanent relationship, you shouldn't have sworn the leinship.' Sehereden was right but being offered unconditional love had been too precious a gift to refuse. 'Fariye says you deny being Valen *or* Astraali,' continued Sehereden when Viv said nothing.

'That's correct.'

'That you told Fariye that or that it's true?'

'Take your pick.'

'She also said you were searching for your mother. *Are* you searching for your mother?' asked Sehereden, choosing his words more carefully this time.

'Yes.'

'How long is it since you last saw her?'

'A while.'

Sehereden grunted and Viv smiled grimly. With a bit of luck, he would soon be so annoyed with her he would off load her. But if he *were* annoyed, he showed no sign of it. 'Larger settlements such as Esh-accom use traders or coin as payment, but in the vals, trade is the commonest way to acquire what is needed. There are things I need to know about you and I'm guessing there are things you need to know about Esh-accom. Shall we trade?'

'There's only one thing I need to know,' said Viv.

'And that is?'

'Why you're the lein of an arsehole.'

'An *ars-hall*?'

'The source of all things quarash.'

He stiffened and Viv searched for a landing place in case she must dodge a fist, but again his voice remained even. 'Leinships are often forged through adversity,' he said. 'When I was fifteen, I was caught by a maragh. Ataghan came to my aid. I lost my knife in the boar's first charge, and Ataghan lost his in its second. We killed it, but it could have killed us. We swore the leinship that night, covered in its blood and our own.

'There are things Fariye's told me about your time together and others I've guessed. It's irrelevant whether Fariye is Ataghan's seed-child or his choose-child. In being *his* child, she acquired his strength. It helped her survive before you found her and after you were lost to her. In swearing a leinship with her father, I chose well, as I believe Fariye did, in choosing you.'

Viv grimaced, resentful Sehereden's little speech had left *her* feeling like the arsehole. 'As I've answered your question, it's fair you answer one of mine,' he said after a while.

'Ask away,' said Viv, and braced for questions about the Waradi.

'How old are you?'

'Eighteen.'

'Where were you raised?'

'That's two questions.'

'It is indeed. Your turn,' said Sehereden.

'Do you have children?'

'No.'

'Why not?'

'That's two questions,' said Sehereden lightly.

'Touché,' said Viv.

'*Tooshay*?'

'It means you just evened the score. You've also used your question, so it's my turn again.'

'Touché,' said Sehereden and laughed. 'So, do you still want to know why I have no children?'

157

'Yes.'

'I've no lein- or si-tryst and have yet to be favoured as a choose-father.' Viv deduced seed-children resulted from some sort of marriage-like arrangement, but she had no idea how choose-children were acquired and did not ask. Sehereden's tension was obvious, and she knew that violence often followed when men were challenged.

They went on in silence, but the horse's ears flicked back and forth, and Viv guessed Sehereden communicated with it. She was considering what Poss had said about Eshadi horses being the most sensitive, when they turned up the valley's side and the horse's back suddenly tilted.

'Hang on to me or at least to my jacket,' he said, as she began to slide. 'Once we reach the ridge top you can let go, if you want.'

Viv held to his jacket, but it was loose, and she had to grip him around the waist. He smelled of leather and horse and was hard-muscled under his clothes. As the arsehole's best bud, he would have done a lot of fighting, she reminded herself, but his physical closeness reminded her of how long she had been alone.

At least the ridge top was too exposed to hide attackers and as an added advantage, it was alive with birds. 'We'll give Fara a short rest,' said Sehereden, and taking her wrist, lowered her to the ground.

He instructed Fara to stay near, turned back, and stopped. Viv watched the leaf-lilters, her face filled with delight, and Sehereden stared. He had never seen an elddra look anything but grave before, *morose* was how they were usually described, and he wondered if Viv's animation were due to youth. Elddra were said to live over a hundred zadicans, although no one knew for sure, and at eighteen, Viv was just a child in their terms.

But not in the Valen's terms, not with the festivities so close. He watched her as he unwrapped the retsen Tahsin had given him and added it to the cheese he had brought from Esh-accom. 'Do you want to eat?' he asked.

'No,' she said, but she did sit nearby which surprised him. Very little on this trip had gone to plan. Return the bracelet, express his regrets, and leave. He had not expected her to have healed, or to have enough affection for Tahsin to agree to travel with the *arsehole's* lein. Nor had he expected the Waradi leader to continue his pursuit, *if* he had. Tahsin believed so and he was no fool, and that made their journey back even more hazardous.

But some of his expectations *had* been met. Fara's images of fire and darkness confirmed her hatred and fear of him and images of still water confirmed her love for Fariye but those of birds showed a surprising playfulness when they had traded questions. Eshadi horses were highly sensitive to the nuances of their riders, but Sehereden had no need of Fara to sense Viv's emotions shift during the morning. Her hatred of him had lessened, although it stayed strong for Ataghan, and her fear of him had shifted to fear of who might follow.

There were red-haired women in Eshavale, but not with skin and eyes such as hers. Viv's gleaming curls framed a face that was a curious combination of child and woman. She had a child's broad brow but a woman's sensuous mouth and, in the bright morning light, her eyes were so deep a blue as to be almost purple. His lein's acerbic observation that Sehereden had a preference for blue eyes was true, but he also wanted to make amends for the injuries he and his lein had inflicted.

He broke off some retsen and lured a leaf-chitter closer to peck it up, then handed Viv a piece and watched her do the same. 'Leaf-chitters are greedier than leaf-lilters,' he said softly. 'You won't tempt a lilter anywhere near as close.'

Viv's attention was on the leaf-chitter that had pecked up the furthest crumbs and she held out the last fragment until it took it from her hand. 'See how easily even wild creatures are tricked into trusting?' she said.

Her voice held challenge but Sehereden was distracted by the curve of her throat, exposed by her open jacket, and *bereft of amé*. And then, as if to underline the perilousness of her state, Fara's head came up. 'Get down,' he ordered, relieved when she obeyed. He crouched in front and drew his knives as Fara sent an image of a snake.

Horses did not differentiate between threats and Sehereden did not know whether the image heralded attack, a storm, or the stench of something dead. The image faded but Fara remained restless. 'Time to go,' he said, packing up the food and mounting. 'I said earlier it was a three-day ride to Esh-accom, *if* nothing went amiss,' he said, as he pulled Viv up behind him. 'A lot of that route is through icestone country, which is treacherous, so we'll take a different route. It might take a couple of extra days, but it should be safer.'

'Why have you changed your mind?'

'I've just told you it's—'

'You knew that before. What's happened?'

'Nothing's happened, I've just decided—'

He felt movement behind him, and she was suddenly on the ground, glaring up at him. 'I'm not some bloody package to be delivered, Sehereden! I've spent a lot of my search for my mother on my own because I wasn't told what the hell was going on, so when the shit's hit the fan, I've ended up wearing it!'

Viv's demand to be kept informed was clear but not much else was, except the suggestion she had travelled with a companion which confirmed what Poss and Esh-accom's elddra said. 'What's changed is that Fara's uneasy,' he said.

'How do you know that?' Sehereden briefly outlined how Eshadi horses communicated their feelings and was relieved to see Viv's anger ebb. 'So, it could be a dead bird *or* a murdering mob of Waradi?'

'Yes.'

'I'm betting on the latter, in which case, it's best we go our separate ways. I don't want anyone risking their neck for me.'

'No!' he exclaimed and joined her on the ground. 'If there's a debt, it's mine.'

'The arsehole's you mean.'

'We're lein so it's the same.' Viv's mouth twisted, and he searched for a more persuasive argument. 'I'm not speaking of debt but of common sense. It's a quicker journey on horseback and safer, especially as I know the way and you don't. That's why Tahsin put his trust in me.'

Her eyes narrowed as she considered him. 'Trust is a pretty slippery commodity, Sehereden.'

'Not in my hands.'

'You're not going to be different to every other man I've ever known, are you?'

Her tone was scathing but her words suggested she *wanted* him to be different but as he considered how the light lit the violet depths of her eyes, a familiar throb started in his guts

'If every other man you've known was untrustworthy, then yes, I am,' he said. She half shook her head but the sense that she *wanted* to trust him strengthened as did

161

the importance of Tahsin's warning. 'I've answered your question as to why our route should change,' he said. 'The trade is that you continue with me.'

'For a while,' she replied.

Chapter 26

Sehereden scanned for signs of ambush as they cut nightwise across the vals, but he also searched Fara's images for Viv's feelings, in the hope of better understanding her. She searched for threats too but when he named the birds they passed, or spoke of their nesting habits, the images Fara conjured changed. They did not represent happiness exactly, but they were close.

Viv's pleasure in even the commonest birds was puzzling, for elddra disliked birds, and he considered Fariye's claim that Viv denied her Astraali *and* Valen parentage. It was possible her mother had lied about her father and raised Viv in a val where she had not learned the elddra's distaste of birds, but if so, Viv would identify as Valen. It was a question he was determined to resolve but not until her trust had strengthened.

Their travel necessitated steep ascents and descents and, as Viv pressed against him and her fragrance permeated his senses, he pondered Valen claims that elddra scent-marked to trap men *and* that they spied. Men were not maragh boars and the Astraali had no need of spies, given they could visit the Vales any time they liked but the slurs ran both ways and his lip curled as he recalled Anfarena's assertion Valen lovers could not meet an elddra's needs.

Viv's charge that men were untrustworthy, suggested she'd *had* Valen lovers and if Fariye's childish understanding were correct, still had a Valen lover, in the form of the mysterious Thrisdane. At least Thrisdane's existence confirmed Anfarena's claim elddra did not live or travel alone, although Anfarena had not countenanced a *lowly* Valen as a worthy companion.

The light was fading when Fara sent the image of a snake again. The land's openness did not favour attack, but clouds billowed above the ridges, and Fara's unease might stem from those. The storms in cloudwise vals could be sudden and violent, and while Amethen's sett was close, it might not be close enough.

'Fara's worried?' asked Viv, when Sehereden drew his knife.

Sehereden nodded skyward. 'I hoped to reach a starwise sett for the night, but we need to find shelter now.'

'Are there caves nearby?'

'There should be.'

He instructed Fara to hasten but the stallion had barely started up the slope when rain squalled down, and the ground was soon awash. Fara stumbled, righted himself, then slid several lengths on his haunches before he managed to stop.

Sehereden caught Viv's wrist to stop her falling and jumped from the stallion's back, taking her with him. He kept hold of her as he reclaimed the pack and instructed Fara to seek shelter below, then shifted his grip to her hand and set off upslope. The cliff face promised caves, and as he struggled on, a smudge of darkness emerged from the murk.

He thanked Enda but as soon as they reached the cave, Viv wrenched her hand free. Fara had granted him a curious form of mental intimacy with her and, while he understood her physical rejection of him, it still jarred.

He dumped his pack at the cave's back and busied himself building a fire using oilstone and the windfall that had blown in. Brilliant flashes of blue illuminated the sky behind him, flinging his shadow against the back wall as

Soaich flung his Bolts, and Sehereden again thanked Enda for the cave's safety.

He added a bigger piece of windfall to the fire, knowing they must dry their clothes and warm themselves, then glanced back and froze. Viv was standing in the cave's entranceway, *fully exposed*.

'Viv!' he screamed, but too late. A Bolt hit the cave's lip, exploded in a shower of phosphorescent sparks, and hurled her almost to his feet. He beat out the smoulder of her clothes, and though she still breathed, she was rigid.

Sehereden knew of only one instance where someone had survived a Bolt strike, but they had suffocated. Viv's ribs flexed like bellows as she fought to breathe, and Sehereden clamped his mouth over hers, and forced air into her lungs. Her terrified eyes told him she was aware, and he kept rhythm with her heaving chest as he forced in more air, then wrenched off his amé and tossed it over her head. Its guidance would be imperfect, but it was all he had.

Sehereden laboured on through the night, keeping rhythm with her attempts to breathe, and slowly she was able to take more air for herself. Her skin was icy, and he shifted her closer to the fire and stripped off her wet jacket. She wore her shirt strangely, with her back exposed, which at least made massaging her easier and he kept up a reassuring monologue as he rubbed her back, shoulders, arms and legs, to aid her circulation and then finally, her breathing fell into the even rhythm of sleep.

Sehereden slumped back on his heels, eyes shut as he thanked Enda, then tucked a dry jacket over her, put more fuel on the fire, and slept too.

Viv was woken by a pain so savage she cried out and Sehereden was crouched and armed in an instant. 'I don't have any atze,' he said worriedly, as he sheathed his knives, 'and it's too late in the zadican for it to grow so far cloudwise.'

'How long does the pain last?' she gasped.

'I've got no idea. I've never known anyone to survive a Bolt strike. What in Enda's name possessed you to stand in the open?' Viv shut her eyes to avoid answering. She had thought the brilliant blue spheres pretty variations on the cat creature's coloured stars, and on the fireworks back home. Sehereden's footsteps rasped away, and as the pain tore through her, she curled into a ball and finally fell into an exhausted sleep.

The pain had sunk to a throb when next she woke and Sehereden sat propped against the cavern wall, the firelight making his resemblance to Rim unnerving. The flickering light glinted off his stubble and showed the lines on his face, etched by weariness, and she thought of Thris's unbearded, unlined face. Sehereden's was a human face with human vulnerabilities, while Thris's was angelic, with all the perfection that implied. And yet it had been Sehereden who had fought through the long night to keep her alive.

Sehereden's eyebrows rose as she stared at him and she looked away. 'You look like someone I used to know,' she muttered.

'Friend or enemy?'

'Enemy, as it turned out. Handsome on the outside and rotten on the inside.' Sehereden grimaced and Viv managed to sit up. 'I'm not saying you're the same,' she said.

'So, I'm handsome inside and out?'

Viv reached for her jacket. 'Thank you for keeping me alive,' she said, as she struggled into it.

'Don't thank me for that!' Sehereden's vehemence surprised her as did the fact he had given her his amé. He had obviously thought she would die, she concluded, as she handed it back, and if she had, he would have sent it to the pyre with her leaving himself unprotected. It was an act of selflessness as powerful as Thris's defence of her from the cat creature. 'You need to replace yours,' he said urgently, as he put it on.

'That isn't possible,' said Viv, unsettled by the insight.

'It doesn't have to be exactly the same, remember.' Viv stared at the fire as if troubled by her lack of amé but all she could think of was the gulf between Sehereden and his arsehole of a lein. 'Hungry?' he asked, and Viv nodded. 'So elddra do eat sometimes,' he said, handing her retsen.

'I need to eat after I've been hurt.'

'And have you been hurt often? Or do I have to trade for the answer?'

Viv shrugged and took a bite of retsen, expecting a barrage of more difficult questions but heard music instead and looked up in surprise. Sehereden played a palm-sized version of the Scharii's drum.

'Do you like music?' he asked.

Viv nodded, but in truth it had been Lettie who liked music and it was the memories of seeing her mother happy that Viv liked. 'It's like the Scharii played,' she said.

'Theirs is the *yu-angar* and this is just a *yu*.' He smiled. 'The Scharii live by their playing but they use the yu-angar to speak to each over long distances too. The yu's not nearly as powerful. When we reach Esh-accom, you can choose a yu from a tune-wright. They're not hard to play.'

167

Viv would not be in Esh-accom long enough to choose *anything* but said nothing and Sehereden put the yu back in his pack and retrieved something that flashed in the firelight. Viv stiffened. It was the Waradi tryst-bracelet.

'I came to Tahsin's sett to apologise for the injuries I inflicted, and to return your bracelet. I sincerely regret what you suffered at my hands,' he said formally, and held it out.

'It was at your lein's hands,' said Viv, making no move to take it. Sehereden obviously tested her loyalties to her *Waradi lover*, she realised with a sick, sinking feeling.

'Leins are one.'

'Did Poss tell you how I came by it?'

'Yes.'

'And do you believe her?'

'It's an unlikely story,' he said and placed the bracelet on the stone between them.

Viv was surprised by the depth of her disappointment. *The handsome man's not as charmin' as ya thought, eh Vivi?* Rim's voice intruded. She snatched it up and struggled to her feet. 'I'll need it to trade for food in Esh-accom,' she said. 'I've got an urrut collar and leash to trade as well. I might even make a profit from my time in this shit hole.' She went to the cave's entrance and stared out, angry by how close she was to tears.

'I told Fara to wait near the rill,' said Sehereden evenly, coming to her side. 'I won't summon him until we're closer. I don't want to alert others to our presence. And Viv, I never said I didn't believe you.'

'I don't care what you effing believe,' retorted Viv and strode off down the slope but Sehereden called to her to wait and she stopped. His order not to go off on her own made sense, but it infuriated her to obey.

There was no sign of Fara at the rill and Sehereden whistled softly, waited, and whistled again. The stream's ripple and splash were the same as those at home, as was the smell of wet foliage. If this fold had not been at war, she might have been happy here, but it *was* at war and there was no sign of her mother *or* of Thris.

'Fara's close,' said Sehereden softly, 'but we don't have a lot of daylight left. There's a starwise sett where we can stay, or we can search for another cave, or use the maark.'

'We should keep moving,' said Viv her gaze on the stream.

'Are you sure you don't want to go to the sett? It'll be warm and dry and you're still recovering from injury. The sett leader's hospitable too.'

'To Valen perhaps but no one likes elddra.'

'You told Fariye you weren't of the Astraali.'

'Correct,' said Viv, and heard him sigh.

'You never answered my question about where you are from.'

'That's because the answer doesn't matter!' she exclaimed. 'The Scharii decided I was elddra, bound and slashed me. *Your* lein decided I was a Waradi lein-tryst and sent me into the ice-fire. The Waradi leader decided I was something he could take and so he took me. *You* decide what I am, Sehereden, everyone else has.' She looked past him to where Fara emerged from the trees. 'Your horse is here.'

'I know,' he said quietly. 'It's time to go.'

Chapter 27

Sehereden did not need Fara's images to know Viv saw the tryst-bracelet as a trap. It had condemned her before, and he should have foreseen her reaction. The sunny images of yesterday had reverted to the darker ones, but he suspected he was not entirely to blame. The tryst-bracelet had reminded Viv of the Waradi leader too.

The man had come close to Ataghan's blades by refusing to relinquish her which had strengthened Ataghan's belief they were lein-trysted. His lein was rarely wrong but the images of fear and hate Fara sent, leant weight to Tahsin's belief Viv's contact with the Waradi had been forced. Tahsin also believed the man still hunted her.

Ataghan always planned for the worst turn of events, and Sehereden had developed the same habit. *If* the Waradi leader had shadowed them from Tahsin's sett, he'd had ample opportunity to attack but must still get Viv back to his Vale and she would slow him, even if she went willingly.

The Waradi would also be weakened by living in hiding and need to be very sure of his aim to kill Sehereden with a single knife throw or risk a fight with a wounded Valen and a lover who might side with the man he sought to murder. Given the images Fara sent, Sehereden did not think Viv would side with the Waradi, but he preferred not to test the theory.

If the Waradi *did* shadow them, he would attack where there were few Eshadi setts and the journey back to his own Vale was safest and they journeyed through such an area now! Fara's ears flicked uneasily, which was a bad sign, and Sehereden's guts tightened. Viv rode behind which meant any knife throw was more likely from the front.

'I think the chance of attack is high,' he murmured, over his shoulder. 'Hold to me in case we must gallop. We're headed for Amethen's sett. If we *are* attacked, stay on Fara. He'll take you there.'

'The Waradi's after me, not you. It's time we parted.'

'No!'

'You evened the debt by keeping me alive when I should have died. I'm not having anyone killed for my sake.'

'You think I'm such a poor fighter?' he whispered, trying to make light of it.

'He puts a knife in you, there won't be a fight.'

Fara's head filled with the blackest images Sehereden had ever seen but before he could react, the Waradi dropped from the trees in front of them. Fara reared but Sehereden registered which foot the Waradi favoured *and* which hand, even as he noted his ragged gauntness. The Waradi's blades were in his hands, as were Sehereden's, but if both threw, both perished.

'You have something of mine, Eshadi,' the man growled. 'Hand it back and I'll be on my way.'

'He's right,' said Viv clearly, and before he could stop her, she slid from Fara's back.

'Viv, no!' cried Sehereden.

She turned back to him, blocking the Waradi's aim, but his aim too. 'It's time I went back to my lein-tryst,' she said, and flicked open the buttons of her jacket. Then she walked slowly towards the Waradi. Viv still blocked Sehereden's aim and the images of birds Fara sent were so distracting he slammed his mind shut.

The Waradi's blood-shot eyes burned into his and Viv was almost to him before they flicked to her. It was only for an instant, but Viv threw herself sideways, and Sehereden hurled his knives. Viv heard the Waradi's sharp exhalation as the knives thwacked into him, then the wet slice of Sehereden's blade across his throat.

The Waradi gurgled and thrashed on the ground and as her legs gave way, she crawled to a patch of aromatic foliage and vomited until her belly was empty. Sehereden did not even glance in her direction, let alone offer comfort, just collected windfall. Viv struggled to her knees and wiped her mouth. Maybe Sehereden blamed her for having to kill. He heaved the Waradi's body onto the wood he had collected, placed the dead man's blades in his hands, and used oilstone to ignite the fire.

Viv buried her nose in her collar as acrid smoke filled the trees, reminded of the arsehole's massacre, but Sehereden remained motionless at the pyre's head until, as the temperature dropped, Viv crept closer to its warmth. 'The Waradi *was* your lein-tryst, wasn't he?' he demanded, his hard gaze on her.

Viv blinked in confusion. 'I only said that to give you the chance to kill him.'

'Don't lie to me! It's clear from what Fara sent!'

She knew Sehereden communicated with his horse mentally but had not known the horse passed on her thoughts as well. Even so, the accusation made no sense. 'What did Fara send?'

'The same images as when we talked about the birds yesterday. The same *happy* images! You wanted to go back to him, didn't you? Back to your stinking lein-tryst!'

'Which is why I helped you murder him,' she retorted, but she saw how her thoughts had been mistaken. She had only controlled her terror by visualising flying away which Fara had interpreted as birds, but Fara had the simple mind of a horse. Sehereden did not and he *knew* her.

'Maybe you decided I was a better bet,' he continued bitterly. 'Cut your losses with the Waradi and take up with an Eshadi.'

Viv stared at him in disgust. What a bloody idiot she had been! This man not only shared Rim's face but his mean-spirited heart too. 'I've lived as a thief since I was fourteen, *arsehole*,' she said furiously, 'and let me tell you something. The things you pick up in the dark aren't always what you think they are. A diamond ring can turn out to be glass, and a gold box can be tin. Remember that, *arsehole*, before you steal someone's thoughts.'

She yanked the urrut collar and leash from her pocket. 'This is you and your lein's gift to me. Take it back. I don't want *anything* that belongs to you!' She flung it at his feet and swung away but then men stepped from the trees. Their clothes shared the arsehole's patterning, but she was beyond caring whether they were friends or foes. 'This effing night just keeps on getting better,' she muttered, and turned her back on them.

Their leader's exchange with Sehereden told her they had seen the smoke and come to investigate; were excited Sehereden had dispatched the Waradi leader; and that their sett's leader, *Amethen*, would want to hear the details for himself. The man's tone told Viv the invitation could not be refused but they had been heading to the sett in any case.

Sehereden came to her side to repeat the man's message but she ignored him, *and* the hand he offered for her to mount Fara. Someone stifled a laugh, presumably at the *mighty* Sehereden being rebuffed by a *lowly* elddra,

173

and he dismounted again, most of the men on foot anyway.

He walked beside her, and the men's leader, *Drasen*, walked on Sehereden's other side. The two kept up a conversation that ranged between urrut pastures, trade, and tournaments but Viv ignored both of them, and when Drasen asked her name, Sehereden had to supply it.

Fara followed behind and Viv concentrated on insulting descriptions of Sehereden in the hope the horse would pass them on, but as the night deepened, despair replaced her anger, and she hugged herself. The Waradi had loosed the rats of memory and she doubted even Thris could help her heal this time.

Amethen's sett was far bigger than Tahsin's but no lamps burned in the windows, unsurprising given how late it was, and most of the hall's tables were empty too, only the men who Drasen led joining the sett leader, Amethen, for the meal.

Amethen was a giant of a man with a florid face and a hunger for all the news Sehereden had to offer. His questions started with the Waradi incursions, moved onto the Ascadi's, and then canvassed likely Genessi alliances. He asked about the Sylds' meeting in Esh-accom and Sehereden's lein's thoughts on the fighting. In fact, Amethen asked so many questions about the arsehole, Viv realised the arsehole was some sort of leader of the Sylds as well.

Beyond asking her name and offering her food, Amethen ignored her, which suited Viv, as did his questioning of Sehereden. She learned more about the fold during the meal than she had in her entire time there. The tournaments appeared to be a sort of mini Olympics held at Fire Zadic along with a carnival called the *festivities*.

Fire Zadic was only twelve days away but Viv would be long gone by then, in fact, she saw no reason to even linger the night, given Amethen expected Sehereden to put in a guest appearance at *their* tournament tomorrow.

She waited for a gap in the conversation and then addressed Amethen directly. 'I'm a stranger in these parts of the Vale,' she said. 'Is Esh-accom far from here?'

'Two days by horse, three on foot. It's an easy enough journey when the murdering filth stay on their sides of the crests.'

'Is it straight starwise?' she asked, ignoring Sehereden's glare from across the table.

'Cross the next ridge nightwise and follow it down,' said Amethen. 'The Mira-ril joins the Eshacade cloudwise of the walls.' He yawned noisily. 'The sett's full of those visiting for the tournament, so I've billeted you with Ithreya. Teletha's fetching her now so you won't get lost.' He clapped Sehereden on the shoulder. 'We want our champion to be fresh for the tournament tomorrow. I'll show you to your rooms,' he said, but Sehereden did not move.

'I beg your patience a moment longer,' he said. 'I need a few words with Viv.' Amethen nodded and moved away and Sehereden came to her side of the table. Men still lingered over their meals and he kept his voice low. 'You're not to leave on your own,' he said. Viv made no response and he leaned in closer. 'Do you hear me? I want you to stay here until the day after next. Amethen's sett has many who journey to Esh-accom and we're to travel together.'

'You can travel to hell, for all I care, arsehole.'

Sehereden's expression remained unchanged. 'I want your word, Viv, that you won't go on alone.'

'*My* word?' she said angrily, making no attempt at quietness. 'The word of an elddra lein-trysted to a Waradi? Why the hell would you want that?' The men at the next table had given up all pretence of eating and she noted Sehereden's annoyance with satisfaction.

'I want it because Waradi and Ascadi still roam the vals, and it's not safe for you to go on alone.'

'Oh, it's *perfectly* safe for me, arsehole. I'll just find another Waradi lover and *any* Waradi lover is a *better bet* than you!'

Sehereden lowered his voice still further. 'You're a *guest* in Amethen's sett and to leave early would insult the entire sett. And, as I brought you here *and* my lein's a Syld, the insult would extend from him to the Syld who represents *this* sett. Disharmony amongst Sylds aids our enemies and risks the lives of all Eshadi, including children like Fariye. I'm asking you again, Viv, for your word that you won't leave early.'

'Whatever I *choose* to do, arsehole, rest assured I won't risk my lein,' she said.

Sehereden's brows drew as he tried to decipher her pledge and Viv became aware of a young woman hovering nearby. She was wrapped in a blue robe that matched her eyes and her unbraided hair tumbled in blonde curls down her back. Ithreya, Viv guessed, dragged from her bed to collect her.

Sehereden rose and bowed and Ithreya introduced herself and welcomed Viv, but her attention was all for the arsehole and Viv gaped. She had never seen a more blatant display of sexual interest in her entire life, and Sehereden seemed equally smitten. Viv glanced at the men opposite, expecting to see resentment, but their attention was on her and as she followed Ithreya out, she began to wonder exactly what the *festivities* entailed.

Chapter 28

Ithreya's room confirmed that not only was Amethen's sett many times bigger than Tahsin's, but many times richer. The polished wood of the bedheads; the brocade of the bedding; and the beautifully worked silver brush and comb sets; were as opulent as those in Ezam's Haven. Ithreya had the large room to herself, but it was partitioned by a latticed screen to give a second bed privacy when needed. There was even an internal washroom.

Ithreya did not hide her surprise at Viv's lack of belongings and was soon trawling through a clothing chest and assembling a neat pile of clothes. Blue seemed to be her favourite colour with the Eshadi patterning on the cuffs and hems picked out in darker hues.

'I had these when I was younger and about your size,' she said as she eyed Viv critically. 'I'll find a pack so you can take them with you. They'll look wonderful with your magnificent eyes and you'll be even more desired during the festivities.'

'Thank you,' said Viv, genuinely grateful for clothes that were not dirty and scorched, and determined to be gone *before* the festivities.

'Teletha says half the men believe you're Sehereden en-Scinta-ril's lover and the other half that you were the Waradi's,' said Ithreya, her blue eyes fixed on Viv. 'Of course, your relationship with Sehereden en-Scinta-ril is no one's business but your own, but I don't want to cause upset.'

Viv blinked, taken aback by her bluntness. 'The men are wrong on both counts,' she said. 'Sehereden *en-Scinta-ril* is all yours.'

Ithreya's warm hands unexpectedly gripped Viv's. 'Thank you. Many women would lie, especially for Ataghan en-Scinta-ril's lein.' She dropped her voice. 'Sometimes Enda grants atunement early and there's so many other women in Esh-accom.' She smiled. 'Do you have all you need? There are drying clothes in the washroom and there's still warm water. Is the bed suitable?'

Ithreya was obviously keen to be gone but Viv was touched by her kindness. 'Elddra don't sleep much, Ithreya, but it will be good to be clean. Thank you for the clothes. It's very generous of you.'

'Being unable to dream must be hard,' said Ithreya gravely, 'but I'll still wish you a good night.'

She disappeared around her side of the screen, but the gaps in the lattice revealed she dusted herself with what Viv assumed was perfume, and then seemed to pray, arms by her sides, hands open as if she asked for something. If it were for good sex, her prayers might be answered, conceded Viv, given Sehereden's care of her in the cave, but then he might turn on Ithreya afterwards too.

At least Viv no longer had to worry about the Waradi rapist. *Yep Vivi, tick him off the list of the hundred other things that might still kill ya.* Viv scowled. Yeah, Rim, like the *other* arsehole whose daughter she loved, the folds full of sand and cat creatures, and all the witch-burners out there in various guises.

The washroom's bath was more of a large metal bowl than a bath, but big enough to sit in and the water *was* warm. The sett must have some sort of plumbing, Viv concluded, as she luxuriated in the water. She washed her hair, despite it staying shiny and sweet-smelling since her angel part had roused. Her water-straightened curls reached to her shoulders but her hair had been jaw-length

179

at Jimmy Wright's funeral and she was shocked to realise she must have been gone at least a year.

The time in Ezam had taken on a hazy, dream-like quality, with Thris its only concrete reminder and *if* a year had elapsed, she had missed her birthday. 'Happy birthday, Viv,' she whispered.

Poor Vivi; no cake an' candles to celebrate? *No gathering of friends*? Viv scowled as she wandered around her room. She longed to unbed her wondrous wings again, in an in-your-face rebuttal of the suspicion she generated, but she was pretty sure she had drawn the Waradi last time and there was already a tension in the air she did not want to add to.

The whole sex thing in the fold was odd. No woman asked another woman permission to have sex with a man they both fancied, and men did not ignore outsiders making plays for their women, or they had not in the gangs. And she had no idea what *atunement* was and how or why Ithreya wanted to get the jump on her competitors in Esh-accom.

She stopped and stared sightlessly as the wall. Maybe she had underestimated Sehereden's popularity, and she travelled with Esh-accom's second most eligible bachelor, after the powerful Syld, Ataghan *en-arsehole*, of course

Viv's mouth twisted. Sehereden's relationship to the arsehole, and the arsehole's relationship to Poss, had certainly complicated her life. If Poss's da had just been one of the ordinary men here, Viv would already be on her way to another fold *or* embroiled in another disastrous uncountable possibility of the Rynth!

Ithreya did not return until close to dawn, and then she crawled into bed, pulled the covers high, and slept. If she and Sehereden had been at it all night, he was not going to perform very well at today's tournament, concluded Viv cynically. The smell of wood smoke suggested the kitchens were operating and sick of her room's confines, Viv decided to escape to the eating hall.

She dressed in her new clothes and smiled, pleased to be rid of her ragged ones, brushed out her hair with a silver-handled brush, and examined herself in the matching hand mirror. Her reflection reminded her how much she looked like Thris, and she stared at the image hungrily. He was beautiful, and Viv had been called beautiful too, but she had never trusted compliments and flipped the mirror over, hoping to see angels, but saw flowers instead, replaced it on the chest and tiptoed from the room.

The smell of cooking led her to the hall where others ate, and she was part way across the wooden floor before she noticed she was the only woman there. The men stopped eating and Viv forced herself on to an empty table near the window, where she could pretend to be fascinated by the view.

Prenya had brought trays of food to the door but Viv had no idea how things worked here and did not want to look like a *haughty* elddra who expected to be served. She was not hungry anyway and was considering escaping outside instead when Drasen appeared bearing two steaming bowls and presented her with one.

The daylight revealed Drasen to be about Sehereden's age but fairer, with hazel eyes and brown hair. 'You look very well this morning, Violet Iris Vacia,' he said with a smile, 'and not nearly as angry as last night. Or maybe your anger will return with the re-appearance of Sehereden

181

en-Scinta-ril?' He paused, but Viv said nothing. 'Usually it's Sehereden en-Scinta-ril's lein who elicits such strong emotions, not Sehereden himself,' he added. 'You've met Ataghan en-Scinta-ril?'

'Yes.'

'And is Sehereden better or worse than his lein?'

Drasen's tone might be bantering but Viv sensed he tested whether her romantic relationship was actually with the arsehole. 'It would be an improvement if his lein wasn't on something,' she muttered.

'*On* something?'

'Things that are drunk or smoked that make people aggressive,' said Viv reluctantly, wishing she had kept her mouth shut.

'The Stonash smoke *tiru* to fortify themselves against the Grey Fire but I know of nothing that produces the effects you describe. Of which val do you speak?'

'Moonsun,' mumbled Viv, staring at the gorash as if she had never seen stew before.

'Moonsun?' repeated Drasen. 'On which rill is that?'

'I—' began Viv, but fortuitously another bowl of gorash chinked down on the table and Sehereden settled beside her. His dark hair shone, and he smelled of soap, but it was his demeanour she noticed, so familiar from the gangs she had coined a term for it: *cat in the sun*.

How often had Rim lounged in the doorway of a squat and smiled lazily at her after a night of sex with someone new? Sehereden did not taunt her like Rim, but he sat so close their thighs touched, and he was like Rim in that way too. Rim did not want her, but he would not let her go either. *Ya like an effing drug*, he would say, each time he came back to her.

'The blue suits you, Viv. You should wear it more often,' said Sehereden.

Viv extended her fascination with the sight of stew to its taste and having her mouth full gave her an excuse not to reply. The air frissioned between the two men and Viv sourly concluded Drasen was annoyed Sehereden had claimed a sett woman but refused to share his own.

'We were discussing what your lein might be on,' said Drasen conversationally. 'Viv thought he might drink something that caused aggression. I was just saying I'm unfamiliar with such things, but you're obviously far closer to your lein than I am.'

A ripple of tension ran along Sehereden's thigh. 'I know of nothing either, but as Ataghan will be at Eshaccom's tournaments, you might like to ask him yourself,' he said evenly.

Drasen laughed. 'I don't think I'd dare,' he admitted. 'It was Viv who suggested it, so maybe she'll ask, *if* she's brave enough.'

'I think Viv is brave enough for anything,' said Sehereden, and rested his hand lightly over hers on the table. 'It was her courage that allowed me to kill the Waradi leader.'

Drasen straightened. 'I've not heard that part of the story.'

'Nor will you today,' said Sehereden. 'I know Viv still finds it distressing.'

Viv managed to swallow the mouthful of stew but had no stomach for more. Sehereden was telling her he no longer believed she was in league with the Waradi, but she did not care what the arsehole believed and jerked her hand free. 'I need some air,' she said, and strode from the hall.

Chapter 29

The air was certainly fresher outside and Viv pulled it deep into her lungs as she struggled to calm. It had taken Thris countless hours to teach her to control her anger, but the Waradi had destroyed his work in seconds, and Sehereden's betrayal then casual expectation she would trust him again, infuriated her.

People made their way towards the hall for breakfast and Viv searched for an escape route, but Ithreya appeared before she could move. 'The blue *does* suit you,' she said, with a smile. 'Have you breakfasted?'

'Yes.'

'I've heard that elddra find crowds disturbing,' she said more softly. 'Would you like to see the sett? It's quiet this time of day.'

'You've yet to eat,' pointed out Viv.

'I can eat later,' said Ithreya and looping her arm through Viv's, led her away down one of the many paths. Viv was unsure she wanted company and then she jumped as a bell sounded and Ithreya patted her arm. 'The early tournaments have started,' she said. 'These are for the boys. The men's and finals are later this evening. We'll take a quick look.'

Viv had imagined the tournaments would test the Valens' skills in things like riding, knife-throwing, and running, but there seemed to be only one activity and it was similar to wrestling. The competitors stood on opposite sides of a sand-filled rink, and on the sound of a bell, sprinted forward and grappled until one was tossed to the sand. The whole thing was over in seconds and the winner competed with the winner of the next round until there was an overall winner.

They wore the briefest of loincloths and slicked their skins with a tart-smelling oil Viv found repellent and she was glad when Ithreya led her away towards a dense stand of trees. They were like those she had seen in Poss's sett but there was no smell of burning here and no Scharii waiting to pounce, just countless birds crested with red, green, and yellow plumage and Viv gazed up at them in delight.

'Mottlecrests favour the aphra,' said Ithreya. 'There's plenty of scharii for them during Cascade but come Lirium, the flocks shift starwise and feed off the britha in the redrin groves instead.'

Viv nodded, as if she were familiar with *britha* and *redrin*, and they went on, emerging from the trees' deep shade into a patchwork of sunny vegetable gardens and orchards. The sett was more extensive than she had realised, and she wondered how many people lived there.

Ithreya described the urrut grazing lands higher in the val as they walked, and chatted about the likelihood of good harvests, then stopped when they reached a rill she called the Verra. The path went on towards forested hills but Ithreya settled on a stone seat positioned to give a pleasant view of the water. There was a holding pool further up the slope, she explained, that provided for the sett's needs via stone-lined channels.

Ithreya patted the seat beside her, and Viv reluctantly sat and braced for questions. 'Sehereden's told me you search for your mother,' began Ithreya. 'Valen children live with their fathers and are used to their mothers coming and going as they please but the elddra replace the love of *both* parents with the love of other elddra.' Ithreya glanced at her sideways. 'You look so sad, Viv, I wonder whether you search for your mother because the fighting robbed you of your elddra companion.'

Viv felt like telling Ithreya to mind her own business, but she had filled a lot of gaps in Viv's understanding and her concern for Viv was genuine. 'When I was ten, I was told my mother had died, and when I was eighteen, I was told she hadn't,' said Viv briefly. 'I want to find her, that's all. I'm only going to Esh-accom to say goodbye to Po— *Fariye*, then I'll resume my search.'

'It must be hard to have no choose- or seed-father,' continued Ithreya. 'Unfortunately, the Du-Daimon don't seem to care about the children they seed. It's one of the reasons the Astraali shun them.'

'I thought they were all Astraali,' blurted Viv and bit her lip. As an elddra, she should know such things.

'They're spoken of as if they are,' acknowledged Ithreya, 'but my seed-father was fascinated by them and I share his interest. He managed to piece together what happened after the Angellus departed.'

'The *Angellus*?' echoed Viv. She had not heard of the Angellus either and their name was too similar to *angels* to be a coincidence.

Ithreya nodded. 'The Angellus weren't always at the sacred mountain of *Ourassin* but no one knows where they came from, or when, for that matter. Nor is it known when and why they left. Only the Scharii and Stonash frequent Ourassin without being *Called*, and the Valen who *are* Called, do not speak of the sacred lake's gifts.

'My father was Called and when he returned, he sought out others who'd been Called,' continued Ithreya. 'From what he saw for himself *and* learned from others, he concluded the Angellus had returned to their homeland.

186

The Angellus were said to be very beautiful, winged, and long-lived. My father believed the Angellus were drawn to Ourassin's lake. Its waters are the most glorious blue and feed the eight cades that give the Vales life. The mountain and its lake have always been sacred to us and we all hope to be Called there one day.

'The Angellus were male,' went on Ithreya methodically, 'and so looked to the Vales for the mothers of their seed- and choose-children. These children called themselves the Astraali and named Ourassin's mountain and lake after themselves.'

Viv's hands clenched as her thoughts raced on ahead. The Astraali were actually daimon then, and *not* angels as the Angellus probably were and, given what she knew of Ezam, Ithreya's father was likely spot on about the Angellus being drawn by the lake too. The Wheel's symmetry would have helped as well, but none of it explained why the Angellus had upped and left.

'When my father was Called,' continued Ithreya, 'he said the Astraali were rarely seen or even spoken of and it was *their* children, the *Du-Daimon*, who patrolled Astraal's streets and managed its trade.'

For the first time, Ithreya's voice took on a hard edge. 'Regardless of whether those of Ourassin are Du-Daimon, Astraali or even Angellus, they persuade the most beautiful of the Vales' women who answer the Call to stay.' Viv chewed her lip as she wondered suddenly whether Tarchen's animosity stemmed from losing a lover to the Astraali. 'Then they seed children with them, many of whom are condemned to being settless,' added Ithreya. 'It's why there's so much interest in you, Viv.'

Ithreya's china-blue eyes were intent, and Viv's heart thundered. 'In *me*?'

'The Astraali are half Angellus, and the Du-Daimon half Astraali, and given their Valen mothers, their seed-children carry very little Angellus blood. Some probably even live in the Vales unnoticed, but you . . .' She smiled again, obviously keen to avoid offence. 'You are like the Angellus returned, except of course, you're female.'

'But there are other elddra,' said Viv wildly.

Ithreya nodded. 'And given their age, most likely seeded by the Astraali. They live with their companions and keep apart, and they are old now, even for those who carry Angellus blood. They are not like you. It's probably why Esh-accom's elddra are so keen to know more about you.'

Tahsin had said something similar, and Viv pushed her hand through her curls. The odds were shortening she should high-tail it down the nearest rift.

'Sehereden was keen to know more about you too. It's why he sought out the elddra in Esh-accom,' continued Ithreya.

'He sought them out?' said Viv hoarsely.

'He wanted to find out more about the particular elddra who saved the life of his lein's daughter, but they knew nothing of you.'

Ithreya paused, obviously expecting Viv to provide some sort of explanation and when she did not, changed tack. 'Sehereden tells me you've sworn a leinship with his lein's daughter. That's also unheard of among the elddra.'

'Why, because we're so despicable?' snapped Viv, rattled by the revelations.

'I didn't mean to imply that but if I did, I beg your pardon.'

Viv touched her hand. 'You've no reason to apologise, Ithreya, you've been very kind to me. It's just that ...'

Viv took a shaky breath. Since being classified as elddra, she had been treated with hatred, suspicion and contempt and she wondered why the elddra did not simply stay in Astraal. Perhaps Valen blood in Astraal was even more of a curse than angelic blood in the vals. The classic half-caste predicament, she concluded grimly.

'Just what?' prompted Ithreya.

Ithreya asked for Viv's trust but Viv had never had many female friends. Her classmate's mothers did not want their daughters to mix with the child of a drunk, and the gang's women had seen her as a competitor.

Birds broke from the trees ahead and Viv flinched. 'It's just some of the men,' said Ithreya reassuringly. 'Those assigned to the urrut pastures return every third morning, or every second during Fire Zadic. No man wants to be absent from the sett then,' she added with a smile.

There were five of them, four about Sehereden's age and an older grey-haired man. They spoke as they strode along but fell silent when they noticed Ithreya and Viv. Ithreya returned their greeting but Viv searched for escape routes. The rill blocked access to the trees and it had been a rill that helped the Waradi catch her. Cold sweat oozed down her back and she felt Ithreya's cool hand on her brow.

'Elddra are known for their good health,' she said. 'Is it possible you carry?'

'Carry?'

'A child.'

'No, it's not possible,' said Viv. The one thing she had never regretted in her shitty life was being infertile. Rape was appalling enough without conceiving a child and she had seen too many skinny children in the squats dragged from dirty bed to dirty bed by women unable to care for themselves, let alone anyone else.

'You don't want a child?' asked Ithreya, in surprise.

'Not if they must live as I do.'

'If you had a child with Sehereden, it would live in Ataghan en-Scinta-ril's sett. There are many comforts there and the val is rich as well as beautiful. A child growing there would have a happy life.'

Ithreya was obviously unaware the arsehole's sett was a pile of ashes, but what puzzled Viv was her willingness to extoll Sehereden's virtues given she wanted him for herself and Sehereden had pretty obviously been more than willing.

'I must get back,' said Ithreya. 'I'm helping prepare tonight's feast. Amethen's festivities are small compared to those in Esh-accom, but it's good to celebrate as a sett before some of our members depart.'

'I might keep walking,' said Viv, and Ithreya nodded.

'The path splits a little further on and if you're looking for solitude, take the nightwise path that leads up through the aphra and marly stands and, if you want a *really* long walk, right up to Mirrina Ridge.' Ithreya patted her arm. 'We've had no trouble in our val, Viv, but it would be best to stay this side of Mirrina and be back by nightfall or Sehereden will come looking for you,' she added with a smile.

Ithreya's words might have been light-hearted but they were probably true, thought Viv acidly, as strode off. She turned nightwise and started to climb. She glimpsed urrut herds on the pastures below and forests beyond them and then entered another stand of trees. Ferns sprouted in moist pockets and there were birds by the dozen, their songs filling the air, and their feathers as bright as sumi.

'Only one thing missing,' she murmured. 'And that's you, Thris.' She stared up through branches, willing him to glide down on his magnificent wings, but the air remained empty of his glorious presence.

He *must* have sensed her resonance when he had rescued Ky from the pig-bear, she told herself for the umpteenth time, and *must* be on his way back, unless . . . There were dozens of reasons why he might not return, many of them fatal, but there was also the fact that a moment in Ezam could mean years here, or *zadicans*, whatever *they* were.

Viv broke into a jog to ease her frustration and quickened her pace until she sprinted. She had run like this before the Waradi and as the horror surged anew, she screamed her distress to the trees, using the foulest words she knew, even those her mother had banned.

Breath tore from her lungs and she focussed on a tree at the very top of the ridge, taller than the rest, but its branches were set high off the ground too and she half ran up a neighbouring tree instead, and scarcely slowed as she climbed hand over hand until its branches meshed with the taller tree's, and then she leapt across.

The tree was more difficult to climb, but she used the skills she had honed with Thris and did not stop until she reached its crown. She was dizzyingly high, the rill reduced to a silver thread, the sett revealed only by a puff of smoke. Smaller vals were visible to either side, and the soaring crests of ridges that bound them.

The sacred mountain glimmered in the distance, Ourassin or Astraal, and she mulled over what Ithreya had told her, especially about the Valen women who chose to stay there. Ezam's angels were attracted to women who resembled the Iahhel, like Lettie, *and* herself, for that matter. If Lettie *had* come here *and* experienced the

191

mysterious Call, she might still be in the city in the clouds, and the only way Viv could find out, was if she braved the mountain herself.

Chapter 30

Viv stayed in her perch until the sun began to set. The leafy bower reminded her of the gums where she had sought safety as a child, but she also had plenty to think about, including her reception in the Astraali city, *if* she went there. The Angellus were long gone, but they and their descendants hardly sounded admirable, in fact, they reminded her of Kald.

The Angellus had flown in, hijacked the Valen's most sacred site, claimed their most beautiful women, and flown out leaving their descendants to rule. Not *flown*, Viv corrected, *transited*.

Her heart quickened. It meant there *was* a way out of the fold, or there *had* been. The niggling worry had lodged in her head that she was stuck here because she had fluked a transit *between* different sectors of the fold rather than out of it. There was no guarantee the rifts the Angellus had used were still open, or would open in her lifetime, but she refused to dwell on the possibility.

Ithreya's father had probably nailed why the Angellus had come but why had they left? She could not imagine Kald or Dejon quitting Ezam, but they had not invaded a fold already inhabited, or if they had, no one had mentioned it.

Anything was possible, she supposed, or rather, anything could be part of the *uncountable possibilities of the Rynth*! She smiled sourly and glanced back at the peak, pink in the sun's last rays. If she waited, it might turn violet, and she recalled her mother holding her up to the kitchen window to watch Mt Silvercrest change colour. It was a memory steeped in love and she knew that, whatever the dangers, she could not leave this fold without confirming her mother was not in the Astraali city.

Climbing the tree had been hard in daylight, but going down was many times worse, especially in the dark. She resisted the temptation to fly down and by the time she had reached the ground, the Cascade Zadic lit the sky. It would have been smarter to wait for it, she thought dryly, as she set off.

Viv was in no hurry to re-join those at the sett, despite Ithreya's advice to be back before nightfall. She kept to pools of shadow but glanced up often to enjoy the zadic's fireworks. She might have paid a big price for leaving Moonsun, but there were compensations, not all of which were strange. Owls glided through the branches, and the night was full of their calls, but her enjoyment of them ended when she reached the rill and saw a figure near the stone seat.

She flicked open her jacket buttons then recognised the arsehole's lein. 'It's late, Viv. I was about to search for you,' he said.

She thrust her hands into her pockets and strode on by, but he fell into step beside her. 'I'd have thought you'd be too busy servicing your fans,' she muttered.

'*Servicing my fans?*'

'Making love to the queue of women at your door, presuming you won the tournament, of course.'

'I did win, for the competition here isn't strong, but there'll be time later for any gifts that might be offered. In the meantime, my concern is for you. I want to make things right between us.'

'Don't bother, I'm just passing through.'

'Searching for your mother or searching for Thrisdane?' he asked. Viv looked at him sharply. 'Fariye told me about him. She seems to think you're lein-trysted. Are you?'

'I'm lein-trysted to the Waradi, remember.'

'I must beg your pardon for that mistake,' said Sehereden. 'It's what Fara sent as you approached the man that caused my error.'

'It's the slipperiness of trust!' she retorted.

'Trust can be rebuilt, if there's a willingness.'

'And betrayed again.' No one had rewarded her trust, including her mother who had *chosen* to leave, and Thris, who had attacked her in Moth Fold, then cared for Ky later at her expense, but then her thoughts turned to Poss. It had taken a long time for the little girl to trust her and then she had committed to Viv whole-heartedly by swearing the leinship. Now Viv was to break that trust by leaving. She had warned Poss from the start she could not stay but it still felt like a betrayal.

Sehereden did not speak again until they reached the sett and then only to suggest Viv join the festivities, and when she declined, to tell her to be ready to leave at dawn. Viv resisted the urge to say she would leave when *she* felt like it, and he escorted her to the room she shared with Ithreya and wished her a goodnight.

She could hear music and laughter from the hall and part of her longed to join in, especially as there was dancing, but Sehereden had not denied his tournament win would give him a choice of sexual partners, and she suspected the sex would not be confined to him.

Viv had seen no flirting, kissing or touching at the sett, but it seemed to be open season when it came to actual sex. There was no reason why it should not be, she supposed, but it would be really handy to know how this fold operated.

She could just imagine the conversation. *You see, Sehereden, I came down this iridescent tunnel into your world while, in actual fact, I'm still in my own world, standing at the graveside of the thug I thought was my father, except he wasn't. So, if you could just explain to me how your society works, and the Astraali city, which I need to visit in case my mother also arrived down an iridescent tunnel and decided to stay, I'd be very much obliged.* Somehow, she did not think Sehereden's much vaunted trust would stretch that far.

Ithreya did not return until close to dawn and then went straight to the washroom and emerged dressed in a jacket and trousers, her loose hair braided, and carrying a pack. 'Are you ready?' she whispered through the screen.

Viv collected the pack Ithreya had given her and followed Ithreya out into the dewy air. Ithreya looked happy, having no doubt enjoyed a lot of dancing and other *activities* with Sehereden during the night, and Viv wondered how weary she would be by day's end. It depended on how many rest stops they had, she supposed.

Ithreya told her they were to breakfast at the Mira Rill, which Viv assumed was in the next val, so it sounded like they were in for an easy ride. There were only three women in the group of twenty, herself, Ithreya and a stout, grey-haired woman who already protested at having to mount.

'We discussed last night, Nurana, that this was to be a riding party,' cajoled an equally stout, grey-haired man, 'and you know Basa's happy to carry two. Now give me your hand. We don't want to be the cause of any

196

delay.' Nurana was hauled on board, still protesting, and Drasen and Sehereden urged their horses forward. Ithreya immediately took Drasen's hand, to avoid an awkward situation for Sehereden, assumed Viv, and she allowed him to pull her up behind.

The party set off along a leafy path beside the rill and the water and the gentle air made for a pleasant start to their trip. The path was wide enough for Drasen to ride alongside and Ithreya kept up a commentary on everything they passed. Apart from the man Viv guessed was Nurana's lein-tryst, the men looked to be the same age as Sehereden and Drasen. Off to test their luck in the tournaments and in the *gifts* that *might* follow, deduced Viv cynically. At least the men in this fold seemed to take responsibility for the pregnancies they caused, unlike Kald. If he had looked after Lettie, there would have been no Jimmy Wright, no years of abuse, and no growing up on the streets.

'Are you unwell, Viv?'

Ithreya's clear blue eyes were filled with concern and Viv shook her head and made an effort to calm her expression. Drasen looked across too but Sehereden had no need to, the flick of Fara's ears telling him her thoughts, and she determinedly concentrated on the birds.

The horses turned down the bank, picked their way across the rill and started up the next ridge. The steep windy path meant they must go in single file, the silence broken only by Nurana's squawks and the soothing murmurs of her lein-tryst. They reached the ridge top and immediately descended again. Viv slid hard up against Sehereden's back, his nearness waking her need for comfort as it had before and in desperation, she thought of Poss but felt no better.

It would be a mistake to visit Poss if she had forgotten about Viv and the horrors of Esh-embrin and settled back into her old life. It might be better if Viv just went on her way except it would mean another fight with Sehereden *unless* she slipped away while he ogled Ithreya. On the other hand, she had pledged Poss never to leave without farewell and Poss was only a couple of days away.

She was still debating what to do when they reached the Mira Rill and the party dismounted. Fires were set and a cheerful hum of conversation soon filled the air. Sunlight shafted through the smoke as retsen rounds were fried in something that made Viv's mouth water, and she accepted a round and ate it as she watched the rill's pristine flow. 'You look thoughtful,' said Sehereden as he came to her side.

'I'm considering my options.'

'Which are?' Viv said nothing, her eyes on the water. 'You'll be with Fariye again soon,' said Sehereden softly.

'I want to see her again, but after?' She shrugged.

'*After* is even better. You'll live with us in Ataghan's sett.'

'That sett no longer exists.'

'We'll rebuild it to be even more beautiful than it was before. You'll be happy there, Viv, and so will Fariye, with her lein.'

Sehereden narrated some sort of bloody fairy tale and Viv decided to test the *happy ever after* bit of the ending. '*Your* lein won't agree.'

'You've not a had a good beginning but time heals many things and Fariye's happiness is important to At, as it is to me. He'll want you with us for *her* sake. And I,' he added softly, 'will want you with us for my sake.'

'What? An elddra?'

'Yes, an elddra.'

Sehereden's dark eyes were intense, and she looked away. It was bloody typical he shared Rim's handsome face and then she noticed Ithreya's gaze was on her too. Ithreya's want of Sehereden was genuine and she had been kind, but what of Sehereden's motives? He probably wanted to add her name to his list of conquests, just after Ithreya's. 'I've told you before I'm just passing through,' she said.

'It might be time to stop, Viv. To make a home, to let love grow.'

His words were like a knife in the wound of her needs, and she rounded on him angrily. 'Is that what Fara told you I wanted?' she demanded.

'Horses only pass on simple images which is what contributed to my earlier mistake,' he said and paused. 'But your sadness, fear and uncertainty are confirmed by what your face shows.'

Sehereden's words stayed with Viv the rest of the day, despite her knowing that living happily ever after with him and Poss was closer to Cinderella's story than her own. But she was tired of being alone, of being a stranger in strange places, and common sense told her the chances of finding her mother were zero. And even if Thris returned, their search had hardly been a howling success. Face facts, Vivi; ya might just have had the best offer ya ever likely to get.

And yet she dreaded ending up like her mother who had traded her body for food and shelter, and nor would she wait in line for Sehereden's attentions like she had with Rim. And then there was the arsehole, who would always be wherever Poss was. If only Thris would come back, it would solve everything!

Chapter 31

Thris could not remember a time when he had not been bound, when his world had not consisted of a cage so cramped, he could neither stand nor lie down, when bitter substances had not been forced down his throat. In his more lucid moments, he realised the mixtures dulled his senses, but nothing could dull his pain. The cage and his bindings made harmonising impossible, and the endless days of disjoint pushed him ever closer to madness.

His captors had blurred into an amalgam of cruel words and crueller actions. When he first roused, they had prodded him with sharpened sticks, standing on opposite sides of the cage so he could find no escape. They wanted him to fly, but despite their torment, the risk of revealing his angelic nature was too great. The sticks had given way to blades and then, one day, they had set a fire in the bottom of the cage.

Ezam had no fire, except that confined by the Red Helixai, and its ferocious pain had sent his wings bursting from his back. He had smashed against the cage in a berserk attempt to escape and they had tossed water over him to extinguish his burns and left him in peace for a time to heal but there had been no kindness in their faces, just a satisfaction that filled Thris with dread.

They had returned sometime later to strip away the soiled remnants of his clothes, dress him in cloth that covered only his genitals, and daub him with oily blue and purple paint that glittered with silver and gold. Then they had hauled his cage atop a wheeled device drawn by animal caste, thrown something heavy over the bars that blocked all light, and an endless jerking and rocking had begun.

His captors stopped to eat and sleep on their journey, and to force more potions down his throat. They kept him bound, and he sank ever deeper into a pit of agony that was so far from the stars, that he yearned for death.

Ash plunged through the Green Helixai's fetid darkness but felt no fear despite the rush of steamy air past his face. It was akin to being in a rift, with the rift's bright iridescence replaced by a velvety darkness, and he landed as if he had stepped from a rift too.

The ground was hard beneath his feet, not sodden like the surface above, and all he could see was stone. He had searched for a tunnel and found one, but it was vertical not horizontal. In places, the walls glowed a deep emerald, as if the stone were lit from behind by a human caste lamp, but in other places, the stone's darkness was impenetrable.

He sensed for resonance and for anything else that might aid him as he crept forward and while he doubted the Green Helixai would gift him music, he knew *something* waited for him here. After a while he noticed great woody ropes twisted down the walls and as he went on, they thrust through the ceiling too until it was like walking through a forest. But there was no bright shine or tinkle of silver and gold here, just a scent Ash puzzled over as he walked. It was not the rank odour of the plant caste above but something ripe with the throb of sweetened juices that reminded him of ambrosia.

The stone floor gave way to detritus that muted his footsteps and the illumination in the walls caught the occasional glimmer of something else beneath his feet and he peered down. Jewelled fragments of lacewings lay next to the amethyst husks of scarabs, and the empty shells of mantises mirrored the green of the tunnel walls. Ash's breath hissed as he realised he walked upon layer upon layer of Ezam's dead animal caste.

Scarabs ate the Dendrinai's leaf-fall, mantises ate the scarabs, sumi ate whatever ended up on the forest floor, and then glimmers ate them. How then, did the remains of their corporeal forms come to be here? Ash stared around at the woody forest and his heart faltered. They were roots that reached down from the glis above to plunge on through the layers of death beneath his feet.

The shine of bones joined the remains of husks and wings, and the scatter of delicate skulls and jawbones told him sumi rested here too. And then, beyond the curtain of roots, the tunnel opened into a circular cavern.

The Blue, Red and White Helixai had stone slabs at their hearts, but what confronted him here was an immense pile of bones many times his height and wreathing it in rainbow rings, were hundreds of glimmers. Ash froze as he recalled how Archae Serith had caused the glimmers to attack the shekinah, and how only the Principae's grace had saved her life, and he wondered whether the glimmers guarded a slab buried within the bones.

The Blue Helixai's slab had gifted him the power to alter the Rynth and the Red's a platform to leap into the mountain's heart where so much of his old self had been burned away. After the Red's danger, the White's pristine illumination had seemed safe, but it had been a trap and had taught him that ascendance was not gained by isolation, no matter the beauty of spiritual contemplation, but by action and now he was here, in the Green Helixai's heart, and all he could see was death.

The pile contained the countless fine bones of sumi and the delicate spines of glimmers that must have taken eons to amass and as Ash paced around the pile, he became convinced the slab *did* lay at the pile's centre and of what he must do.

His thoughts went to Ky, safe in the Bokos, and to Thris, deep in the dangers of the Rynth. They had come into being together and he had hoped they would transcend together but that hope now seemed as dead as the bones before him.

He did not know Ky or Thris's paths to transcendence, but he knew the next step in his own, and taking a steadying breath, he began to climb. The pile was surprisingly stable, and he hummed as climbed, scarcely aware of doing so, and the glimmers slid sideways to create an empty bone pathway up the mound. And then, he reached the summit, and his eyes widened in horror.

Other bones lay there, and Ash's trembling hands picked up the skull. Its lightness told him it was angel caste and then he noticed the feathers. They were arranged to enclose the bones like a nest enclosed the eggs of bird caste. There were blue feathers, but the majority were white and as the terrible understanding washed over him, he cradled his head in his hands and wept.

Drasen did not call another halt until dusk, and then the party erected maarks and turned their mounts loose. Viv did not worry the horses would wander, but she did worry that Drasen set guards. Nobody else seemed concerned so she hoped it was usual or that he was just being careful. After they had eaten, the men cleared a makeshift rink and practised their wrestling, but they took to their maarks as soon as the zadic had finished. Viv shared a maark with Ithreya who was soon asleep, but the best Viv could hope for was a doze and even that was hard thanks to Sehereden's offer of a home.

He would have other lovers at the arsehole's sett because there would be women who cared for the men's seed- and choose-children, given their biological mothers did not hang around. The bond between the arsehole and Fariye seemed strong but someone else must have looked after her while he was off killing.

Viv chewed on her lip. Harems were hardly a new idea although the women here seemed to have a hell of a lot more power than the women in the gangs. It was *Ithreya* who had pursued Sehereden, and it was the *women* who chose the fathers of their children, and who *chose* to stay in their setts, or *not* to stay.

Why ya hesitatin' Vivi? Want a man all to ya self? She had never liked sharing Rim, even at his most violent, and it had taken jail, with its enforced hours of solitary contemplation, to understand why. After the loveless Jimmy Wright, she had wanted to be so special to someone, to be so *loved*, that the person would never turn to anyone else ever again. It was the Cinderella-thing again: a Prince who searched *only* for her, a glass slipper that fitted *only* her foot, but it was a hunger now as well. In joining angelically with Thris, she had experienced an ecstasy no man could match and yet Thris yearned for something he could only have if he left her behind.

'Just my shitty luck,' she muttered, and sick of the maark's confines, crawled outside. The fire was deserted, and she settled on one of the stones the group had used as seats. The stars were not bright enough to be the Milky Way and no Southern Cross hung in the sky, but she could still be in Moonsun, and the smell of wood smoke added to the illusion.

'One more night and you'll be in Esh-accom with Fariye,' said Sehereden, making her jump. He appeared in her line of vision, hefted a piece of wood onto the fire, then settled on a stone beside her.

'It must be a coincidence you can't sleep either,' she said sarcastically.

'I've just come off guard duty.'

'Then you should be sleeping,' said Viv. 'You don't want to be tired for the *festivities*.'

'Plenty of time for those, but not plenty of time to enjoy your company alone.'

'It may not be that enjoyable,' said Viv, reminded *again* that Valen men did not bother with pick-up lines.

'I'm sure it will be. May I take your hand?'

'Why would you want to do that?'

'Is that a yes?' he asked with a smile.

'I suppose,' said Viv, with a perverse curiosity as to what he would do next.

He took her hand and turned it over. 'In Esh-accom there are women who claim the palm's markings tell what's passed, and what's to come.'

'And you believe such things?'

'I'd prefer not to. They foretell a short life for me, but I wonder what Viv en-elddra's hand shows. Shall we look?' Viv shrugged and his fingers moved lightly over her palm, making her skin tingle. 'Much travelling, and too much time alone in the past, but a far happier time ahead with those who love her.' He brought her hand to his lips, his kiss on her palm no more than a gentle brush. 'Your skin smells of flowers,' he murmured.

'Be careful it doesn't trap you.'

'Men aren't maragh boars and nor are elddra intent on trickery.'

'What makes you so sure?'

'That men aren't maragh boars or that elddra aren't deceitful?' Viv shrugged again. 'I'll assume the latter. There can be no deceit without lies, Viv, and the elddra don't lie.'

Sehereden's face was as gentle as Rim's in their good times together and her heart quickened as he kissed her hand again and his lips lingered longer. 'Given that the elddra don't lie,' he continued, 'do you think it's possible you will live with me in Ataghan's sett?'

'Many things are possible.'

'I should have asked whether you think it's *likely*,' he amended and leaned in closer, not so close as to be threatening, but close enough for her to offer him her mouth. His sensitivity reinforced her belief he would make a considerate lover, but she knew that some time in the future, Sehereden would tire of her elddra novelty and move on.

'You were right in your earlier summation of me,' she said and extricated her hand. 'I'm not a good bet.'

'We both know I was wrong,' he said, in the same gentle tone, 'but love, like trust, takes time to grow. I am patient, Viv en-elddra. I am prepared to wait.'

End of Angel Caste Book 3 - Angel Bone

Continue Viv's story in: Book 4 Angel Bound

Amazon US - https://www.amazon.com/dp/
B071VBNTSM
Amazon Australia - https://www.amazon.com.au/dp/
B071VBNTSM
Amazon Canada - https://www.amazon.ca/dp/
B071VBNTSM
Amazon UK - https://www.amazon.co.uk/dp/
B071VBNTSM

Take a peek at Book 4

Viv's dread grew as she recalled the previous massacre. 'You won't be involved,' said Sehereden briefly, and Viv realised Fara had communicated her thoughts.

'I'm already involved.'

Sehereden made no response and as time stretched away, Viv's thoughts wandered. And then, all hell broke loose. There were shouts and the pound of horses, and Sehereden urged Fara out of the trees and positioned him midway down the slope. Viv's heart raced as other riders appeared beside them to form a line between the rill and the forest. There was another line of men visible in the dimness ahead. The fighting she heard must be closer to the sett, and she realised the Waradi had been allowed to approach it and been ambushed.

Waradi who escaped and galloped back towards the rill, would be cut down by the line of the arsehole's men in front, and any who escaped *them*, would be finished off by Sehereden's men. Viv gripped Sehereden's jacket, scarcely able to breathe. A riderless horse galloped out of the darkness and the men created a gap to let it go. A second, *mounted one*, followed, and swerved upslope as its Waradi rider saw them. He pounded past Sehereden and Viv, but as the men closed ranks, wrenched his horse back.

The slope was slick and it skidded, went down on its haunches, and cannoned into Fara at speed. The shock hurled Fara sideways and Viv was aware of being airborne, and of hitting the ground. Her face smacked onto stone, the world disintegrated, and then burst back as pain exploded in her arm. She was aware that horses thumped about her, that men grunted as they fought, but then the sounds faded away.

I hope you enjoyed *Angel Caste* Book 3 – *Angel Bone*.
Authors need reviews! It is how our readers find us.
I would love you to leave me an honest review on
Amazon, Goodreads, or another of your favourite reader
sites. Read on to discover my other books.

Works by K S Nikakis
Available on Amazon KDP and a range of digital
platforms.

Non Fiction

**Journey: Seeking the Sacred, Spirit and Soul in the
Australian Wilderness**

Deadway - Finalist Best Poem
2020 Australian Shadows Awards

When we set out into the wilderness, what is it we *really*
seek?

Do we seek new sights or do we seek new selves? And
are we *really* on one journey or on two?

Journeying fifteen thousand kilometres into Australia's
blood-red heart, Nikakis discovers that every journey is
perilous, for travellers risk carrying the clutter of their
outer lives with them; a clutter that blinds them to the
other journey they crave; that of the inner *soul-journey*
into a deeper understanding of self.

To enter Australia's vast Outback wilderness, is to enter
a place of endless horizons; a place doused with brilliant

gold dawns and dazzling sunsets; a place silvered by star-encrusted night skies and, most importantly, a place of hidden sacred places in whose deep stillness our inner journeys can at last unfold.

In the spirit of travellers like Robert Macfarlane and Scott Stillman, Nikakis asks what it is we really see, feel and understand when we follow in the steps of those who have gone before us deep into the wilderness.

Drawing on her Ph.D. in Joseph Campbell's hero myth, and using original poetry and novel extracts, Nikakis takes us on this second journey; a journey of the sacred, spirit and soul, where our inner selves finally have the time and space to gift us richer and more fully-realised lives.

Fantasy Novel Series

Angel Caste 5 Book Series – available complete in one book or as five individual books: Angel Blood, Angel Breath, Angel Bone, Angel Bound, Angel Blessed.

Angel Caste – Complete 5 Book Series - *A modern female hero on a timeless quest*

A troubled street kid, an angel guide, a binding promise . . .

Viv is on day release from jail to attend the funeral of the thug she thinks is her father, when her real father turns up, the powerful angel Archae Kald. If that is not shocking enough, Viv discovers her mother is not dead after all but lost somewhere in the tangle of worlds called the Rynth.

Determined to find the only person who ever loved her, Viv rift transits to Kald's angel world where he assigns the beautiful Thris to guide her to her mother. Thris is different to every male Viv has ever known but after a life on the streets, she finds it impossible to trust.

Thris trains her to travel the rifts, but the Rynth is a dark and dangerous place, even for angels and when Viv's angel traits emerge, disaster strikes. Lost and alone in the Rynth, Viv stumbles on a lost child in a war zone, and pledges to take the child to safety. But in the perilous worlds of the Rynth, deciding who is friend and who is foe is a deadly game of chance.

Bound by his pledge to guide Viv to her mother, Thris embarks on a desperate search for her, but a greater threat confronts them both and they must fight not just for their own lives, but for the lives of those they love.

The Kira Chronicles - 6 Book Series – available complete in one book or as six individual books: The Whisper of Leaves, The Silence of Stone, The Secrets of Stars, The Thunder of Hoofs, The Crying of Birds, The Music of Home.

The Kira Chronicles – Complete 6 Book Series – *traditional fantasy with deep forests and high stakes*

A gold-eyed Healer, a prophecy, two brothers at war.

In seasons long past, twin gold-eyed princes sundered a kingdom. Rejecting his brother Terak's warrior ways, Kasheron led his people deep into the great southern forests and established the healing settlement of Allogrenia. The Tremen flourished, upholding Kasheron's legacy of peace and healing, and protected by the vast, trackless trees.

All Tremen delight in the healing arts, but Kira is the greatest Healer of them all.

To the north of Allogrenia, drought ravages the Shargh's land, and as their suffering escalates, the chief's younger brother seizes on an ancient prophecy to snatch the chiefship for himself. The prophecy links the Shargh's doom to a gold-eyed Healer, and Kira has gold eyes.

The Shargh attack with devastating consequences and Kira must fight to save the wounded, but the Shargh wounds rot, no matter her skill, and Kira finds herself in a deadly race against time. As the slaughter continues, she makes the horrifying discovery that the Shargh hunt

214

her. To halt the attacks and save her people, she sets off for the North to seek aid from her long sundered warrior kin.

But the dangers beyond the forests exceed even the Shargh attacks. The Tremen detest their warrior kin but Terak's descendants have inflicted a worse fate on the Tremen. Kira's new-found love is torn apart by ancient hostilities and when trust turns to betrayal, it risks everything she fought for.

As the battles rage on, Kira becomes increasingly sickened by the bloodshed. Desperate to end the suffering once and for all, she sets out on a quest that could cost her everything and everyone she loves.

Fantasy Novels

The Emerald Serpent – *the Celtic Fae in a fight for survival*

Book trailer: https://www.youtube.com/watch?v=bGpKxnpCEMg

Betrayal, torture, death: Etaine lives on only to destroy those who robbed her of everything she loved.

Seven years before, Etaine met fellow Ranger Cormac, the Eadar she believed was her longed-for true-mate. Emerald-eyed, white-skinned, and black-haired, the Eadar had formed into Ranger bands to fight the Fada, invading religious zealots determined to replace the Eadar's Serpent Goddess with their own gods of stone.

The pure blood of the ancient Eadar runs strong in Etaine and Cormac's veins, and their joining had the potential to open the Emerald and Serpent Ways to them, old worlds only true Eadar can enter. But their love affair goes tragically amiss, with catastrophic consequences.

Etaine flees and as the years pass, slowly rebuilds her life, but the Fada's attacks grow more ferocious, and the Eadar are forced to fight for their very existence. When the Fada mass to commit yet more bloody slaughter, and the bands join in a final, desperate effort to defeat them, Etaine comes under Cormac's command, the very last Eadar she ever wants to see again.

Together they have a weapon that can destroy the Fada, but to use it, Etaine must learn to trust again and Cormac to Remember. And time runs short: the Serpent rises.

Heart Hunter – *a female hunter on an impossible quest*

Fleet is a young Sceadu hunter: skilled, strong, and fast.
She hunts deep into the icy mountains, seeking meat
for her people, for the rains have failed and plunged the
Sceadu into hunger.

Her hunts are hard, but she has much to look forward
to. Soon she will be gifted her air-name by the Sceadu's
shaman, and then she will be a full adult, and free to
marry the man she loves.

But while Fleet is on hunt, the old shaman dies, and the
new shaman visions a very different future for her: cross
the frozen, ice-locked mountains and complete a perilous
quest or lose the man she loves forever.

In a moment of anger and frustration, Fleet commits a
terrible wrong and sets out into the frigid mountains to
atone with her life. In a journey that takes her deep into
the earth's darkest places, into strange new worlds, and
even into Death itself, she discovers that only she can
save her people. To survive, she must draw on every
shred of her hunter strength, and doing the impossible, it
turns out, is just the beginning.

The Third Moon – *science fantasy with a very human quest*

Where does the past end and the future begin?

Haunted by inherited memories of his people's dispossession and theft of their children, Warrain is just twelve years old when the nightmare repeats. But Warrain isn't living on Earth in the 21st Century, he is living on the planet Imago in the far flung future.

Five years before, Station One's Mech's got high on the opioid arrash, and in the bloodshed that followed, Warrain's scientific community were expelled from the Station, his father murdered, and his mother and unborn sibling lost to him.

The scientists carve out a rudimentary Station high in Imago's ranges, and Warrain's friends get on with their lives. Not Warrain; he climbs the Tors to stare down at Station One, dream of his mother and sibling, and plot revenge.

And then one day, everything changes. A third moon appears in the sky, one of Imago's life-forms calls him by name, and disease breaks out at Station One.

When the Mechs visit to seek help for their ill, Warrain seizes the opportunity to deal them a blow they will never forget. But the third moon brings changes that threaten them all and, to aid the life-form whose kind is being dispossessed and slaughtered, he must turn his back on the hate that has long sustained him and find another way to live.

Messenger – *a dystopic future filled with hope*

In a world made deaf by hatred, who will hear the messenger?

Severine's world ends the day her family is murdered. Being raised in the loving community of gay Travelers always marked her as an outsider, but being female puts her in mortal danger. Women are scarce, precious, and hunted.

When chance brings Severine face to face with the father she has never known, he assigns the son of his murdered best friend to guard her. They soon clash. Severine believes all men are violent brutes and Jeph resents his freedoms being curtailed.

An uneasy understanding grows but Jeph is glad to deliver her to the Enclaves, a sanctuary her father has carved out in the mountains for his women and children. But there is no safety in a world broken by war and sickness and when violence follows her, Severine flees to the northern city of Andhaka in search of a home amongst her mother's people. Jeph follows, bound by loyalty to her father, but the north holds terrible dangers for him.

It's been years since Andhaka has welcomed outsiders with anything but bullets, and to survive and to protect Jeph, Severine must learn to use her enemies' weapons against them. As the stakes rise, she comes to understand the horror of her mother's loss, and what drove her father north seventeen years before. His quest becomes her quest, but she hasn't counted on the savage legacy that war and sickness have left behind, or on falling in love.

I Heard the Wolf Call My Name – *gender-fluid shifters in search of home*

Finalist Best YA Novel – 2019 Aurealis Awards

Jax is just twelve years old and in bird-form high above his island home, when it explodes, killing everyone on it. He believes he is the only survivor until ten years later, he comes face to face with his boyhood friend, Matiu.

Matiu is military and the military need shifters for a crucial mission, but Jax refuses. Having spent ten long years burying his bizarre shifter past, he isn't about to resurrect it. But Matiu rouses other feelings too that Jax finds harder to ignore.

As the military ramps up pressure to force Jax's cooperation, he shifts to bird-form and flees to the last remaining island where he crash lands in the middle of Anahera's vision-quest. She searches for her skin-spirit animal to transform her into a protector of her people, and dreams of finding the white-wolf, but finds Jax instead. To save him she must abandon her quest but her kindness only adds to Jax's turmoil.

To decide who he truly is and where he really belongs, he must first confront his painful past, but that isn't the worst of his problems. The forces that blew Jax's island out of existence now threaten Anahera's as well, and he might just be the only shifter who can save it.
And time is running out.

Fantasy Short Stories

The Gift – A Deep Fantasy Short Story #1 – free on my website at www.ksnikakis.com

Excerpt:

Thariel sat for a long time, surveying all around her, as if she ate the world that would soon be memory. Then she took the harness from the mare, and with soft words, thanked her and bade her farewell. Her own feet she turned towards the forest, tossing her face-plate aside as she went, so that her hair fell loose to her waist, then she discarded her chest-armour, the sword and dagger, her bow and quiver.

The trees closed in and she came at last to the lake Men call Menios and stood for a while on its shore. An owl cried and a mouse shrieked, and all around her the souls of the newly dead jostled in their journey to the void. She stepped into the water and the new life inside her quivered.

'Fear not, little one,' she whispered, in her own tongue. 'We are going home.'

The Tale of Prince Anura – A Deep Fantasy Short Story #2 – free on my website at www.ksnikakis.com

Excerpt:

I should have been happy, for she was beautiful. Dark rivers of curls, skin as white as moonlight on water, breasts softer than spawn, and she loved me well. But her chamber was small, no matter the comfort of her bed, and the old feelings of entrapment rose, as persistent as gas that bubbles from rot below still waters.

I sat at the casement and listened, as I had once loitered near the watery skin of the second world and waited. The moon grew large and small many times, but it came at last, as I knew it would. The soft lament on the night-time air, the song of a soul as confined as mine. It took me a journey of many days through the depths of a massive forest to find her tower.

Stone it was and sheer, and as remote as the third world's glimmer had once been. I sang to her and she answered with sweet melodies of her own and we made love as frogs do, with our voices. And when trust had built, she let down her shining ladder of golden hair.

Glass-Heart – A Deep Fantasy Short Story #3

Finalist Best YA Short Story, Aurealis Awards, 2019.

Excerpt:

Geth moved amongst his band, exchanging quiet words while they waited. Some he had fought with since the Tallon's foul ships had first found their shores while others had come later, when the burn of cot and kin had sent them from their valleys.

Hate drove them but hate was no shield against arrow and knife. It was fighting skills that kept them hale, and Geth ensured they had them aplenty. He needed them living, not just for their own sakes and his, but for what would come later. When the Tallon's stain had been scoured away, the destroyed must be rebuilt.

Kyth sat alone and he went to her and gazed about. 'The glass-heart's fled, has it?'

'I sent her to a place of safety. She will come to me when it is over.'

'Safety was what I wanted for you!'

'And what I wanted for Nyar.' Her eyes caught the star-sheen as she looked up at him. 'But you can't always have what you want, can you, Ceannasai?'

Dragon Sprite – A Deep Fantasy Short Story #4

Excerpt:

Genn rocketed straight upwards, not just because she enjoyed seeing the limitless blue sky before her, but because a Waiwin's wing shape made vertical flight harder for them. Orin didn't try to catch her but swept in circles around her, gaining height in an ever-narrowing spiral. It was a clever tactic and one Genn didn't believe hehad thought of in the instant she had cleared the trees. He had obviously studied her strategies and developed a plan to counter them *or so he thought.*

Genn waited until the spiral narrowed to *axeel*, the minimum distance a Waiwin must keep from a Velven unless she *accepted* him, then swerved towards him, narrowing the distance between them. Orin's eyes flashed to black, shocked she *had* accepted him, but before he could act, she folded her wings and dropped.

The strength that had driven Orin's pursuit had surged to his wing-tendrils in anticipation of locking them with hers and he would struggle even to stay airborne until it flowed back.